Candle's Christmas Chair

Jude Knight

Published by Jude Knight at Amazon
Copyright 2014 Judith Anne Knighton writing as Jude Knight

Thank you for your purchase. If you enjoyed this book, please watch your favourite ebook retailer to discover other works by Jude Knight. Thank you for your support.

Dedication
To my husband, who has been my personal romantic hero for 45 years. You taught me how heroes love by being strong, kind, determined, gentle, protective, and caring. Thank you for believing in me and for supporting me.
I love you.

ISBN 978-0-473-31352-4

Table of contents

Chapter one: An unexpected meeting

'Tha' wants to talk to Min about they chairs," said the man in the office, and directed Candle Avery to the far corner of the carriage-maker's yard.

Candle strode through the light rain, dodging or leaping the worst of the mud and puddles. Min. Short for Benjamin, perhaps? Or Dominic?

No, he concluded, as his eyes adjusted to the light inside the shed. The delightful posterior presented to his eyes belonged to neither a Benjamin nor a Dominic. The overalls were masculine, but the curves they covered were not.

She was on a ladder, leaning so far into a bank of shelves that lined the wall opposite the door that her upper half was hidden, but he had no objection to the current view—said delightful posterior at his eye level and neatly outlined as she stretched, a pair of trim ankles showing between the tops of her sensible half boots and the hems of the overalls.

"Botheration." Whatever she was reaching for up there, it was not obliging her by coming to her hand. Perhaps his lofty height might be of service?

"May I help, Ma'am?" he asked.

There was a crash as she jerked upright at the sound of his voice, and hit her head on the shelf above. As she flinched backward from the collision, the ladder tipped sideways, spilling its occupant into Candle's hastily outstretched arms.

The curves were everything he thought, and the face lived up to them. A Venus in miniature, black curls spilling from the kerchief that held them away from the heart-shaped face, that quintessentially English complexion known as peaches and cream, grey eyes fringed with dark lashes.

Grey eyes that had haunted his dreams for three long years, ever since she'd led him on at a house party for the amusement of her friends, and then left without saying goodbye.

Grey eyes that turned stormy as he held her a moment too long. He hastily set her down.

"Miss Bradshaw."

"Captain Avery. No, it is Lord Avery, now, is it not? My condolences on the death of your father."

He bowed his acknowledgement, his mind racing. Bradshaw Carriages. He hadn't made the connection. Had he known when he was courting her that she was a carriage-maker's daughter? He didn't remember anyone mentioning it.

But he did remember that her friends called her Minnie. Miss Minerva Bradshaw. Min.

Lord Avery was broader than she remembered. He'd been little more than a boy at that horrid house party, but even then the tallest man she had ever met. Isolated and nervous in that crowd of scheming cats who had only invited her to humiliate her, she'd believed him when he claimed to care. She'd been thrilled when he called her a little goddess, and asked for leave to worship her.

With him at her side, she'd braved the crush at the ball. Short as she was, she usually found such occasions overwhelming. People looked over her, bumped into her, ignored her. But Lord Avery—Captain Avery he'd been then— kept her safe. She'd even, for the first time in her life, been enjoying herself at a ball. Right up until she overheard his best friend talking to him, and it became clear that Lord Avery despised her common origins and was only courting her for her money.

That had been Min's last venture into the aristocratic world her parents had educated her for. She'd come home to Bath, and told her mother that she would marry, if marry she ever did, within her own class. But none of her suitors had ever measured up to the tall red-headed guards officer who even now, standing here in her workshop, turned her knees to jelly.

What was he doing in her workshop? Why would he track her down?

"Can I help you, Lord Avery?" She couldn't do much about the colour that pinked her cheeks, or the way her heart pounded. But she could, and did, keep her voice level and her tone cool.

He was immediately all business. "I am after a chair, Miss Bradshaw. It is still Miss Bradshaw?"

She nodded, seething. How dare he comment on her marital status. She wanted to tell him that she'd refused five proposals in the last three years. But he was continuing: "The Master at the Pump Rooms told me that Bradshaw Carriages makes the best chairs in Bath, and the man in the office sent me here."

"I see. And what sort of a chair do you require?"

His brows drew together. "An invalid's chair. That is what you make, is it not? What your father makes, I mean?"

He might as well know the whole of it. She was not ashamed. And if his eyes turned cold and scornful, what was that to her? She was, no doubt, just imagining the warmth she saw. As she had imagined his admiration so long ago.

"You were right the first time, Lord Avery. I design the chairs. And I make each prototype for my assistants to copy."

"I say," he said, "good for you!" And he smiled at her. She remembered those smiles. And, though her mind knew he couldn't be trusted, her foolish heart didn't believe her.

Miss Bradshaw was as lovely as he remembered. Such a shame that she preferred other women! He'd refused to believe it at first, when her friend hinted it to him after she had run off. What a fool he had made of himself over her.

"So can you sell me an invalid's chair, then," he asked.

She sighed, and in a patient voice explained, "I need to know more about how the chair will be used, Lord Avery. We have chairs suitable for street use, chairs that work well in a park, chairs that can be easily pushed inside a house, even chairs that can be propelled by the occupant. What sort of chair do you require?"

"I see." That made sense. What didn't make sense were the signals he was receiving. Three years ago he'd been as close to an innocent as a 19-year-old with a father like his could be. But his time in the Coldstream Guards had taught him a great deal, including what to think when a woman's pupils dilated, and she became breathless and flushed.

Perhaps it was wishful thinking. Certainly, his own anatomy had a strong opinion about what to do with the delectable Miss Bradshaw and his own reaction might be predisposing him to misread hers.

Inspiration struck.

"Can you show me each different type and explain what the different uses are, please, Miss Bradshaw?"

There. That should win Candle at least 15 minutes to observe her while she showed him around.

She stood her ground. "Who is the chair for, Lord Avery."

Good point. He needed to remember his key purpose in coming here, which had nothing to do with pursuing the elusive Miss Bradshaw.

"My mother was injured in the same accident that killed my father," he told her baldly. "She is paralysed from the waist down. I wish to buy her a chair so that she is not totally dependent on being carried to go where she wishes."

Miss Bradshaw's lovely grey eyes softened and warmed. He remembered how changeable those eyes were. They could go cold with disdain, hot and stormy with anger, and warm with compassion. Lying eyes. He had to keep reminding himself that she had made a fool of him.

"Ah, your poor mother. Yes, we will certainly find a chair for her. And what sort of places does she wish to go?"

Min showed Lord Avery the inside chairs first. He was very taken with the Merlin chairs, named after the inventor, a clockmaker who had built a self-propelled chair after he'd broken his leg. Lord Avery asked her to demonstrate how to turn the handles on the arms, and then insisted on trying the chair himself, folding his great length in order to fit.

"I think we should have one of those," he said, brushing past her as he circled the chair, examining it from all sides. He skimmed his hands down the chair's sides, gently caressing, and Min's mouth went unaccountably dry.

"Yes, well," she said. "Over here we have the outdoor chairs." She had designed them for different types of surface, changing the size and pitch of the large wheels on either side of the chair, and lengthening or shortening the undercarriage to change the distance between the chair and the small front wheel that the occupant could turn in order to steer.

Once again, Lord Avery insisted on trying the chairs, handing her into each one, parading her solemnly up and down the workshop, and then handing her out. Fortunately, he seemed focused on the chairs, and didn't notice her fingers trembling. His effect on her seemed stronger than ever.

"I like this one," he said, finally, pointing to the one chair they hadn't tried.

"I am sorry," she told him. "That one is not for sale."

"But it would be perfect," he said. "The wheels are broad, so Mother won't sink into the grass when she strolls in the garden, and they are slightly skewed to give her greater stability. The longer undercarriage also improves stability, but it isn't long enough to impair turning, so she will be able to manage even the paths in the maze. It's perfect."

He'd listened to her every word. More; he'd understood exactly what she was trying to do.

"It is a prototype," she explained. "I do not sell my prototypes, and I do not manufacture until the prototype has been thoroughly tested."

He was nodding before she'd finished. "That's even better. Let us test it for you. And once you are satisfied, you can sell us one of the new models."

He took both her hands as she opened her mouth to reply, speaking before she could. "Please, Miss Bradshaw. It would mean so much to her. She used to practically live in her garden, rain and shine. To be able to get there again without being carried; to be able to move around and decide where she wants to go—it would mean the world to her."

His big hands cupped hers; his thumbs stroked across her trapped fingers. For a moment, she was almost mesmerised, but then she tugged her hands, and he released her instantly.

"But you wanted it for Christmas." It was a weak protest, close to a capitulation, and he clearly knew it.

"But this is even better, don't you see? She'll get the use of a chair immediately, without waiting for Christmas, and at Christmas she'll have one made just for her. Oh. But will there be enough time?"

It was late October. Not quite two months to go. Yes, they could do it. Min would need to start building the model before she got the prototype back, but the final testing was unlikely to prompt major changes.

"I will need to upholster the chair and to run some final tests, then your mother could have it for perhaps a month? I will need to talk to her after that."

"Of course. I'm going to take that—did you call it a Merlin? I'll take the Merlin with the red cushions. She loves red. Could you cover the new chair in the same fabric?"

"I could possibly do the same colour," Min agreed. Did she have enough red leather? No; she'd cut the last skin a few days ago. Perhaps she could get some from the main carriage works. If not, she'd have to make a trip to the leather merchants.

He nodded, running a hand over the plush surface of the Merlin and immediately leaping to the right conclusion. "You use leather for the outdoor chairs, don't you? They might get wet, I suppose."

"Minnie, are you in here?" That was her cousin Daniel's inevitable greeting, as if her presence in her own workshop was a perpetual surprise to him. He followed his voice into the room, and drew himself up to his full height, still a good seven inches shorter than Lord Avery.

The man who called Miss Bradshaw 'Minnie' in that familiar way was built like a bull: broad in the shoulders and chest, with massive arms and a thick neck. Candle grudgingly admitted he was handsome enough, in a thick-set kind of way, his blonde hair slightly overlong, square-cut even features, and fine hazel eyes currently fixed on Candle in challenge.

Miss Bradshaw kept her smooth calm. "Lord Avery, may I present my cousin, Daniel Whitlow? Daniel, Viscount Avery is here to purchase a chair for his mother."

The bull relaxed slightly, returning Candle's nod. "Minnie—Miss Bradshaw—designs the best chairs in Bath, Lord Avery." He rested a proprietary hand on Miss Bradshaw's shoulder. "You won't regret choosing one of her chairs."

"Two," Candle said. "Two chairs." How proprietary was this cousin? Not that Candle cared. Not after what she did three years ago. Or did she? If her friend was mistaken about her preferences, did she tell the truth about Miss Bradshaw's reasons for leaving? The bull was saying something else.

"One for indoors, and one for outdoors," Candle explained.

"Daniel, I need dark red leather for the outdoor chair. Can I purchase some from your stock?"

The bull nodded. "Yes, we bought a whole cart-load of skins dyed for the Mail order. We could spare you a skin or two."

"The one you're using is a bit more orange. I had in mind this colour." She ran her hand over the Merlin chair, as Candle had a few minutes ago. In precisely the same place. He wondered if she realised that. He shifted his hat, strategically.

The bull shook his head again. "No. Nothing that colour."

Candle was opening his mouth to say he'd choose another colour when the bull went on, "And I can't spare anyone today to take you down to buy some. We're going to be all hands working late as it is."

"I could escort you, Miss Bradshaw?" Candle offered.

The bull examined him with narrowed eyes.

"After all, the sooner the chair is covered, the sooner my mother can try it out," Candle went on, looking as innocent as he knew how.

It was enough. The bull nodded again. A beast of few words. "Take your maid, Minnie. Your servant, Lord Avery."

Min changed into an afternoon dress in the room her father kept for her in the main building, while Lord Avery waited for her in the office downstairs. He hadn't blinked at the price she asked for the two chairs, writing a bank draft for the first chair, and promising payment on delivery for the other. Rumour had it he'd inherited a fortune from a nabob uncle. Perhaps, for once, rumour spoke true.

As she buttoned her pelisse and tied her bonnet strings, she thought wistfully about the far more fashionable clothes that she had at home. How silly. Lord Avery was a client like any other, and she would no more dress up for him than she would for... she cast about for the person she least wanted to impress. Daniel. She would no more dress up for Lord Avery than for Daniel.

They walked down Cornwall Street into Walcot Street, Polly Stample keeping pace behind.

"How did you come to be making chairs, Miss Bradshaw?" Lord Avery asked. He couldn't really be interested, but she would tell him, since he asked.

"I began when my mother broke her hip, Lord Avery. She was not entirely happy with the chair made by one of my father's workmen, and I designed some improvements. It has grown from there."

"An unusual hobby for a woman," he commented.

A hobby, indeed. Every man Min knew, from her father down, insisted on seeing her work as a hobby. Never mind that invalid chairs were one of their most profitable lines. And she managed it all, from designing the chairs to keeping the accounts.

"It is a business, not a hobby," she told Lord Avery.

He opened his mouth to say something, then visibly thought better of it.

"Go on," she said.

He didn't pretend not to know what she meant. "I don't wish to make you cross," he told her. "I value my skin."

"I will try to resist tossing you into the Avon."

He laughed out loud. "You would need to trip me, Miss Bradshaw. I'm rather too large for you to lift."

"Are you changing the subject, Lord Avery?"

He spread his hands in surrender. "I was just going to say that business is rather an unusual hobby for a lady," he said. "I meant it as a joke, but I decided it wasn't very funny. Truly, Miss Bradshaw, after the last six months, I have nothing but admiration for anyone who can run a business."

He sounded and looked sincere, but it couldn't possibly be true. Min knew what the gentry thought of trade. She'd heard it often enough while she was at school. "Mini, darling, whatever is that smell? Have you not washed today? Oh, but I forgot. You cannot wash off the shop, can you darling?" 'Mini' was short for 'Minimus', a comment on her size, and she hated it.

But Lord Avery was continuing. "I was raised to run the family estate, of course. But I also inherited from my uncle six months ago. He ran a huge business, and now I'm trying to learn how to do it. So far, I've been lucky in my managers, but Mother says I need to know the impact of every decision made in my name, and how everything works, and that seems sound to me."

Min nodded. "That is what my father, says, too. My mother says the same applies to running a house. You have to know how to do everything in order to know everything is being done well. This is Pursell's."

Lord Avery opened the door to the showroom.

At first the sales assistant assumed Lord Avery was the customer, but Lord Avery said, "I am just here to escort Miss Bradshaw."

Min pulled out an off-cut of the velvet they were matching, and leafed through the sample book until she found a match. They didn't have that colour in stock, but she was assured they could have it dyed and ready for her within a week. Min reviewed her schedule. If Lady Avery was happy to trial the chair for three weeks instead of a month, they could still make the Christmas deadline.

"I wish to select the skins," she told the sales assistant.

In the storeroom, she inhaled a deep lungful of the smell of fresh leather, then laughed when she realised Lord Avery was doing the same.

"It reminds me of the saddle room at Avery Hall when I was little," he said. "What about you?"

"My father's harness shop. When I was little, my mother was in charge of it, and I spent a lot of time there. My mother was a Conti."

"Conti? Your mother is related to Gavriel Conti?" Lord Avery whistled. "I am sorry, Miss Bradshaw. That was most impolite of me. But Conti Saddlery is a legend. I have a Gavriel Conti saddle, and I wouldn't part with it for the world."

"Gavriel Conti was my grandfather." She had found the stack of skins she wanted and the sales assistant was pulling them out so that she could inspect them.

The sales assistant's superior attitude changed to reverence when he realised that he was serving the granddaughter of the great Conti. He must be new or he would have known. She seldom bought skins herself, usually picking what she wanted from the manufactory's stores, but she'd been coming here with her parents since she was a babe in arms.

The sales assistant and Lord Avery began exchanging stories about Conti harnesses and saddles that had come unscathed through trials that would have shredded lesser leatherwork.

Lord Avery was not what Min had expected. For a brief week, she had convinced herself that he was not like other offspring of the nobility—that he saw past her modest birth and liked her as a person. Then, for three years, she believed he was just like all the others; an idler who thought his noble birth entitled him to a life of ease and plenty, and who looked down on those whose labours made his leisure possible. Now, he confounded her.

If he wasn't after her money—and if the fortune he had inherited was a tenth of what people said, he didn't need her money—why had he come seeking her? She discounted the story he'd told; it was, after all, highly unlikely the Master of the Pump Rooms would send him to her, of all people.

She would have to watch him carefully, and guard her heart.

Chapter two: Truth in a tea shop

Miss Bradshaw chose the skins she wanted and arranged for them to be dyed and delivered. Out in the street, it was raining again. Candle unfurled his umbrella. He was so much taller than she that if he held it over both of them, she would be soaked in every gust of wind. When he tried to hold it just over her, though, she objected.

"My bonnet will keep me dry, Lord Avery. I must not take you out of your way."

"I promised to escort you, Miss Bradshaw. Surely you will allow me to keep my promise? Do you return to your workshop?"

"I am for home on Henrietta Street. Polly and I will be fine."

Candle turned, and handed the maid his umbrella. One of them might as well be dry.

"Then we will brave the weather together, Miss Bradshaw." He offered her his arm.

They hurried down Northgate Street and turned towards the bridge. Miss Bradshaw leant into him as she jumped over the puddles he strode past. The magic was still working; she still made him feel strong and capable.

Three years ago, fresh out of university and new to the Guard, he'd been nervous in company, expecting the teasing he'd endured at school to follow him into Society. And it did.

But Miss Bradshaw had talked to him about books, and gardens, and animals. She'd listened as he explained his plans for a military career. She'd taken his arm on walks and waved admiringly as he showed off his one skill, outriding all the other male guests.

Tiny though she was, she never made him feel over tall and clumsy. Indeed, she liked his height. She had confided that she was always nervous in crowds, but not when he was there to protect her. Was it all a tease?

On an impulse, he pulled her into the doorway of Crofts Tea House, at the entrance to the bridge.

"Miss Polly," he said to the maid. "Your mistress and I will take shelter here while you hurry home and fetch another couple of umbrellas."

The maid turned uncertain eyes to Miss Bradshaw. Would she agree? Candle held his breath.

"Run along, Polly. We will wait in the tea rooms."

He opened the door for Min as the maid hurried off, almost invisible under the big umbrella.

Following behind, he almost collided with Min's back when she stopped suddenly. He was close enough to feel the tension radiating from her, and the effort she made to relax and continue into the little tea shop.

A servant hurried up. Candle absently asked for a table for two and for tea to be served. Most of his attention was on the couple already seated at the far side of the shop. Guy Kitteridge was one of those who had made his life miserable at Eton and later at Oxford. Kitteridge was with his sister Genevieve, Lady Norton, a slender blonde with a waspish tongue.

They were absorbed in their conversation, and with luck wouldn't notice Candle and Miss Bradshaw. He waved Miss Bradshaw ahead and followed her to a small table near the window that looked out onto the street across the bridge.

Interesting that Miss Bradshaw reacted as she did. Lady Norton had been a great friend of hers three years ago. Although, come to think of it, he hadn't seen any signs of closeness between them during the house party. It was only after Miss Bradshaw left that Miss Kitteridge told him they'd been at school together.

Miss Bradshaw had seated herself so all the brother and sister would see was her back. Candle angled his chair so he, too, would be hard to recognise.

Lady Norton was the one who had told him why Miss Bradshaw left so precipitously. Wasn't that interesting? Candle beamed. Miss Bradshaw raised her eyebrows. No. He would not explain to her why he was suddenly happy. Not yet, anyway. Perhaps one day.

The servant brought a laden tray. Two cups, a teapot, milk and sugar, a three-tier cake plate filled with savoury tarts on the lowest tier, delicate iced cakes on the middle tier, and candied fruit and flowers on the top.

As Miss Bradshaw poured the tea, he tested his new theory. "Mr Kitteridge and Lady Norton are over there in the corner," he said. Yes. That was a slight grimace, quickly controlled. But it was definitely a grimace.

"No doubt you wish to greet your friend," was all she said. But the warmth that had begun to creep into her voice during their afternoon was markedly absent.

"He's no friend of mine," Candle assured her.

"You have had a falling out?" She handed him his cup, prepared just the way he had liked it three years earlier.

"We never had a falling in," Candle said. He was watching the pair from the corner of his eye. They'd seen him—it was hard to be inconspicuous when you were well over 6ft tall and had red hair.

"Don't look now," he told Miss Bradshaw, "but they're coming over."

"Lord Avery? It is Lord Avery. I told Guy it was you." Lady Norton was fluttering her eyelashes at him. She must have heard about his inheritance. Three years ago, she had barely acknowledged his existence, except to show her contempt.

The contempt was well veiled today, at least in his direction. She didn't acknowledge Miss Bradshaw's existence at all.

Well, he could fix that. "You remember Miss Bradshaw, of course," Candle said.

Genevieve Norton, known at school as Kitty Cat, rounded her blue, blue eyes into her innocent look. Min had seen her practicing that look and a dozen others in front of a mirror. "Why, if it isn't little Miss Bradshaw. Fancy seeing you here."

"I live in Bath," Min said.

"Oh, I know that." Lady Norton slid her eyes sideways to Lord Avery, inviting him to join in the fun. "I meant here in a tea shop. With a man. On your own. Oh but perhaps I am mistaken. Perhaps the rules are different for those who are not ladies." And she lowered her voice to not quite whisper to Lord Avery, "She is a tradeswoman you know. Carriages or some such."

He smiled warmly at Min. "As it happens, Lady Norton, you have interrupted a business meeting. Miss Bradshaw is designing an invalid chair for my mother. I know you will excuse us if we continue."

"I know what kind of business I'd like to discuss with Miss Bradshanks." Mr Kitteridge said, waggling his eyebrows at her.

Lord Avery's nostrils flared. She had heard the expression, but she'd never seen it happen. But his voice was quiet and controlled when he said, "Kitteridge, Perhaps you and your sister had better leave now."

Lady Norton fluttered her eyelashes at him again. Practiced expression number 8, or was it 9? "Lord Avery, you must call while you are in Bath. Perhaps tomorrow afternoon?"

"Thank you, Lady Norton. However, I expect to be leaving Bath in the morning."

Kitteridge, his eyes on Min, opened his mouth and then thought better of whatever inappropriate remark he was about to make. He said good day, instead. "Come on, Vivi. Better be on our way. Things to do tonight, you know."

Lady Norton laughed, a tinkling little sound of amusement, also practiced. "Such a busy place Bath is this month, Lord Avery. Tell me, are you staying at the Royal?"

"I am not," Lord Avery said.

"Come on, Vivi. Your servant, Avery. Miss Bradshanks."

Lord Avery took his seat again, and picked up the cup Min had poured for him.

"Do you suppose he gets your name wrong on purpose?" he asked? "Or is it general stupidity?"

The twinkle in his eyes put the nasty couple back into perspective. Now she was an adult, their petty insults had no power to hurt her. She didn't move in their circles, and they weren't respected in hers. Anxiety, indignation: both receded under Lord Avery's calm amusement.

"A little of both, I believe," she replied.

"What a poisonous pair," he said. "Did she make your school days as unpleasant as he made mine? You know, when you disappeared from the house party, she told me that you had just been playing at liking me for the amusement of your friends. Her exact words, if I remember, were 'after all, Captain Avery, you are not exactly the answer to a young girl's prayers, are you?' I shouldn't have believed her, should I?"

Good heavens. She shook her head, her mind racing. Those past few hours at the house party had been too painful to remember, but she was now reliving the conversation that had sent her running to her room, to wait, wide-awake, till morning dawned and she could leave.

"Why did you leave?" Lord Avery asked.

"I heard... I thought I heard you discussing me with Mr Kitteridge. But I have just this moment realised. I heard his voice, but the other voice. It was very low; I assumed it was yours, but... Kitty Cat—Lady Norton—had told me you were just after my money, but she always sees the worst in everyone... And then... Do you remember that I tore my hem and went to have it sewn up?"

"I remember. It was the last time I saw you." His eyes were sombre.

"I came back to the alcove where you were waiting, and I heard Mr Kitteridge say, 'Avery, old chap, you have to admit, if you must marry the shop, it comes in quite a tasty package.' I could not move. I just stood there. I heard someone reply, very low. I couldn't make out the voice or the words, but Mr Kitteridge said, 'That's right, Avery. No need to take her into Society once you've got your hands on her lovely money.'" She blushed, remembering the rest of his sentence, which she wasn't going to repeat. 'Keep her at home and enjoy all her other lovely assets where the smell of the shop won't bother the neighbours. I wouldn't mind getting an heir and a spare on that one, I can tell you.'

"Damn his lying, cheating eyes," Candle said, forgetting for a moment that he was in the presence of a lady. "I beg your pardon, Miss Bradshaw. Will you believe I wasn't there? When you left for the retiring room, I went to get us some punch. I stopped to talk to some people. I was watching the door, but someone..." he stopped, his eyes unfocused for a moment as he remembered. "Lady Norton bumped into me and spilled the punch. I had my eyes off the door for several minutes."

Miss Bradshaw nodded. "She was in the retiring room. She spent 10 minutes telling me how improvident you were, and how unworthy I was, and on, and on—all in that sweet 'I am only trying to help' voice of hers. She left just before I did."

"They planned it. They were in it together."

Miss Bradshaw had clearly come to the same conclusion. Slowly and deliberately, she repeated, "Damn their lying, cheating eyes."

Candle gave a bark of laughter, then turned suddenly serious. "We have wasted a bit of time, haven't we? May we start again, Miss Bradshaw? I was courting you, you know. I'd like to court you again, if I may."

Miss Bradshaw shook her head, sadly. "We come from different worlds, you and I. The Kitteridges were right about that."

"It didn't matter back then."

"I was 17 back then. I believed Cinderella could marry the prince. I did not think about what her life would be like the next morning, raised to scrub out the kitchen and surrounded by people who despised kitchen maids."

Candle would have argued, but the maid arrived with the umbrellas. Miss Bradshaw thanked him for the tea.

"Polly and I will be fine from here, Lord Avery. It is only just around the corner."

Candle insisted, though, on escorting them both to her father's fine terraced house on Henrietta Street.

She gave him her hand in parting, and one of those warm smiles that melted him from the centre. "I am so glad to know what really happened at the house party, Lord Avery. All these years, I have believed I was mistaken in you. I am happy to know that I was not."

He raised her hand, so tiny and delicate in his, but wiry and strong and capable. "Please know that my admiration was, and is, genuine, Miss Bradshaw." He kissed the air above the back of her hand, fighting the temptation to press his lips to her glove—or to strip the glove off and lay his kiss in her palm.

He doused the thought. All unbidden, it had left her sweet palm to travel up her arm and beyond, and he had to remain respectful if it killed him. Any sign that he regarded her as less than a lady would, he was sure, condemn him take her decision on his proposed courtship as final. And that, he had no intention of doing.

Chapter three: A choice of suitors

Mama was in a flap. One of tonight's guests had cancelled, and the table would be unbalanced. The cook had taken back the turbot, saying it was not fresh, had started a screaming match with the fishmonger, and was now sulking. Papa had sent a message saying he and Daniel would be late. And the roses for the dining room were yellow, not pink as Mama had ordered.

Min nodded, and agreed, and nodded again. Mama would work it out. Mama always worked it out, and the dinner would be magnificent, as it always was. But Mama seemed to need the drama of solving one crisis after another.

Min, though she took her colouring and size from her mother, was far more like her peaceful father in temperament. "If you can solve it, Min," he would say, "Then do so. If you can't solve it, it isn't your problem. But worrying never changes anything."

Sure enough, by the time the first guests were announced, the chaos had been resolved and all was in readiness. Mama, with Min at her elbow, presented Papa's apologies for his tardiness.

"A big order. He is upstairs changing for dinner. He and our nephew, Daniel, will be down shortly."

The guest were all from trade families. Several times a week, the Bradshaw dinner table became a location for what Papa called the great game of business. Mama was an even better strategist than Papa, choosing who to invite with an eye to advantage for Bradshaw Carriages, keeping the dinner table conversation light, but providing many alcoves and separate rooms for the private conversations that led to alliances for the benefit of each party.

Martin Billingham, who escorted Min into dinner once her father and cousin arrived, was the son of the man who was trialling them on a Royal Mail order. Mama had suggested the contract might be sealed with a marriage. Mr Billingham was, Min supposed, a nice enough young man. But—whatever the business advantage—Min was not going to marry him.

At dinner, most of the talk was about the French, and whether they would invade. Some of those present believed Napoleon was no longer a danger, now that he was committing troops to fight the Austrians.

Others thought it was only a matter of time until he beat the Austrians and returned to Boulogne.

Min pointed out that the French naval commander, Villeneuve, had combined his fleet with the Spanish fleet, at Cadiz.

"It is a worry," her father agreed.

"Trust Admiral Nelson to deal with them," Daniel insisted.

"And if they don't, we have the militia, do we not?" one of the other ladies said. This was a sore point. The volunteers and the militia needed to be equipped, trained, and paid when they were mobilised.

Mr Billingham senior summed up the general view. "Mark you, it's us that pays when they raise taxes. It always comes back to us trade folk, whether it's windows or servants or sugar. One way or another, it comes back to us." Mr Billingham held the current Royal Mail contract; if Bradshaw Carriages met the deadline with the current order, they'd have a lucrative partnership for the next five years.

"You need not worry, Miss Bradshaw," the younger Mr Billingham assured her, when the men joined the ladies after dinner. "I am confident that Napoleon will not dare to invade. He knows the English will rise up to the last man to oppose the French should they land on our shores."

"Minnie doesn't worry, Martin," Daniel said, taking the seat on her other side. "If the French took over Bath, Minnie would sell them chairs for all the soldiers injured in the invasion, wouldn't you, Minnie? Did you manage to get the leather you wanted?"

"They're dyeing some for me," she said.

"A happy customer then. Although he's not your usual sort, Minnie."

Mr Billingham frowned. "I cannot like you dealing with customers, Miss Bradshaw. The risk! The scandal! I am surprised your father allows it."

Daniel laughed. "Oh Uncle thinks anything Minnie does is exceptional." Was that a sour note? Daniel had no right to be jealous. If anything, the shoe was on the other foot. Daniel was Papa's business heir, and was being trained to take over. Min's childhood dream of running the carriage works would never come true. She knew as much as Daniel, but she was a woman and he was a man.

"Indeed, if I were to have the privilege of taking a jewel such as Miss Bradshaw into my home," Mr Billington was proclaiming, speaking to Daniel rather than Min, "she would never have to lift a hand in any kind of work."

Min and Daniel exchanged glances. Daniel changed the subject. "So who was the long streak? Avery, you said?"

"Viscount Avery. He has an estate a few hours from here," Min said. She knew exactly where it was, too.

"He was buying chairs for his mother." Daniel made a statement of it, a frown creasing his forehead. "I'm sorry, Minnie. I was distracted. I should have sent someone to escort you or asked you to wait till tomorrow."

Mr Billingham looked indignant, his chin jutted forward and his eyes protruding more than usual. "If you suffered insult, Miss Bradshaw, I will... I will seek this viscount out and demand an apology." He nodded as if satisfied with that solution, though the anxiety in his eyes hinted that he hoped such a move would not be necessary.

"Lord Avery was all things gentlemanly, Daniel. Thank you, Mr Billingham. I suffered no insult."

"You must know that I would do anything for you, Miss Bradshaw."

Best to put a stop to that conversational direction immediately. "How kind, but I am well able to depend on my father and my cousin," she said.

Daniel turned a laugh into a cough. "I think my Mama wants me," Min said, suppressing the urge to kick her cousin. "Excuse me, gentlemen."

For the remainder of the evening, she managed to avoid Mr Billingham. She could not keep him from coming to the point indefinitely, but in a few more weeks she would be able to refuse him without any damage to her father's business.

Mama came to tuck her in. "You may be 20, Minerva," she had replied, when Min suggested that she was too old for tucking in, "but you will be my baby girl till the day I die."

"Not Mr Billingham, my love?" she said, as she pulled the sheets up to Minerva's chin and smoothed them out.

"No, Mama. Not Mr Billingham."

"Don't leave it too late, Minerva. Invalid chairs won't keep you warm at night, and you cannot rock business ledgers in a cradle. I know what I'm talking about, baby. Papa and I— Papa was 41 and I was 38 when you were born. We had a happy marriage, but you made our lives complete."

"That is part of the problem, Mama. You and Papa show me that marriage can be a partnership, and I want that. Mr Billingham likes the way I look, but he doesn't like me. He doesn't know me, and he doesn't want to know me."

But Lord Avery does, a small voice whispered. She ignored it. Lord Avery was not for her.

Candle went to dinner with a couple of friends from army days, and they spent the evening fighting an invasion. Beckett was still in the Guard, but their host, Michaels, had sold out about the same time as Candle, and was fascinated to hear that Candle had set up and was training a local company of volunteers.

"If we can hold Napoleon off at sea, we'll be fine," Michaels said. "But we'd be fools to discount the possibility of him landing. And he'll be back when he's finished in Austria."

"It's not like regular army work," Candle explained. "Our farm boys and footmen won't be able to stand up to Napoleon's trained soldiers, and we won't try. But every Englishman and every Englishwoman will be able to strike a blow when the French aren't watching. A broken wheel here, a shot from the darkness over there, a purge in their soup somewhere else."

Beckett winced. "That's hitting below the belt," he joked.

"But you are teaching them to fight," Michaels said.

"Yes, but a different kind of fighting. A few people moving fast in and out of cover, and striking only at weak points."

They spent hours fighting skirmishes and sneak attacks with the salt cellars and the cutlery, taking advantage of every bit of cover provided by a dinner plate or a fold in the tablecloth.

When Candle and Beckett left Michaels' lodgings, the dawn was just lightening the sky. The shortest distance to the hotel district led through the south end of the town, where weary prostitutes returning home from work passed day-labourers heading to the better end of town to begin theirs.

One particularly pretty girl walked towards and then past them, and Beckett turned to watch. "We could pick up a couple of girls... no, you don't do you."

Candle shook his head. "You go ahead, Beckett." He hadn't been with a purchased woman since his 16th birthday, when his father took him to a brothel as a present. That virgin boy had been first embarrassed, then delighted, then—

when he read the contrast between the smile on the painted lips and the hopelessness in the kohl-lined eyes—horrified.

Fortunately, his father had lost interest in him again, and he'd remained nearly an innocent until his disappointment over Miss Bradshaw had sent him seeking experience. He spared a smile for the bored lusty widow who had educated him in London. She was still a good friend; remarried now, and he was glad of it. She deserved happiness.

Her successors had likewise been widows who enjoyed a discrete liaison with someone who treated them with respect and was happy to squire them to social events. He had not had such a liaison in six months; not since he sold out when his father died and his mother was injured. Was that the reason for his lustful response to Miss Bradshaw? He didn't think so. He was all but certain he would respond to her if he'd just been intimate with an army of widows, end to end. And he was completely certain army of naked widows wouldn't have half the effect on him of Miss Bradshaw's delectable posterior in a pair of workman's overalls.

He continued on, smiling at his own besotted imaginings. He could see glimpses of the Abbey. The buildings behind it blocked his view of the river across which Miss Bradshaw would be sleeping. He passed a flower shop that was just opening its doors to offload a cartload of flowers, still in buckets and fresh from the fields. Flowers. Why not?

He was whistling when he exited the flower shop. A wash, a quick nap, a shave, and he'd be as good as new. And in four more hours, when he called to collect the Merlin chair, he would see her again.

Lord Avery was precise to his time, arriving on the dot of 11 o'clock. Min and the worker Daniel had spared to her had the chair packed around with blankets and wrapped in a canvas against the weather.

"My mother asked me to thank you for the flowers." He must have bought every bloom in the shop. They were delivered to her mother; a polite fiction that she appreciated. Min was both appalled at his extravagance and flattered by his attention. "They are lovely, but I told you not to court me," she scolded, when the worker was out of earshot.

"To be precise," he said, "you told me that the Kitteridges were right. This being completely beyond the bounds of possibility, I decided you must be having a momentary lapse of reason, quite out of character, and it would be kindest to ignore you."

"Lord Avery!" She didn't know what else to say. She wanted to laugh, but that would just encourage him.

"You will note, however, that the flowers were not addressed to you, but to the lovely Mrs Bradshaw," he reminded her.

"You have not met my mother."

"True. But I'm sure I would conceive a hopeless passion for her if I did. If I had not already given my heart to her daughter."

"Lord Avery!"

"You could call me Candle if you like," he said.

"I could not."

"You're right," he admitted. "It's a silly name. They gave it to me at school. Because I'm tall and thin and have a flame on top. Call me Randall. That's my name, you know."

Min did know. She had looked him up in Debrett's at the circulating library. She wasn't going to tell him that.

"I will call you Lord Avery," she said, firmly.

"Really? Think about it. You're an efficient woman. Wouldn't Randall be quicker and easier to say?"

"Or Ran," she said, the words slipping out before she could stop them. Sometimes, in her day dreams, she had called him Ran.

Lord Avery was delighted. "Yes. Please call me Ran. That would be very efficient."

"And very inappropriate," she said.

She could tell he was going to argue some more, but the worker called out to say he'd secured the chair on the back of Lord Avery's high-perch phaeton, and Daniel arrived.

Daniel wasted no time. "You sent my aunt a lot of flowers, Lord Avery."

"I did, Mr Whitlow. I wished to show my appreciation for her daughter's help, and my delight that we have met again."

"Is that right? You didn't say you'd met Lord Avery before, Minnie"

"It was three years ago, Daniel."

Daniel turned his suspicious eyes back on Lord Avery.

The bull was very protective. Cousinly? But it wasn't unknown for cousins to marry. Surely Miss Bradshaw would have told him if she had an understanding with the pugnacious Mr Whitlow?

Certainly Candle wasn't going to have another chance for a private word with Miss Bradshaw. His teasing was having the desired effect before the bull butted in. Ran, indeed. He like it. Ran and Min Avery. He liked it very much. And not least because the way it slipped out showed she'd been thinking about him.

"When should I return for the other chair," he asked. "In 12 days?"

"Yes. I'll have it ready by the 6th of November. Shall we say the 7th to be safe?"

As he prepared to climb into the phaeton, the bull crowded in on him, ostensibly to make a hand to give him a leg up. "Be very careful, Lord Avery," he muttered. "My cousin has relatives who will protect her honour."

"I promise you," he said, keeping his own voice low, "I will guard her honour with my life."

The bull looked at him long and hard, then nodded. "Fair enough." And he gave Candle a heave, propelling him up into the phaeton.

Candle leaned down to take the reins from the worker.

"Good day, Mr Whitlow. Your humble servant, Miss Bradshaw. I will see you in a fortnight."

Chapter four: Families have their say

It was a long fortnight. Candle was busy, but he still found time to dream when he wasn't attending to his business interests and the estate, and choosing presents to send to Miss Bradshaw. He wanted her and her family to be in no doubt about his intentions. That meant he couldn't send her anything that would be inappropriate between a gentleman and an unmarried lady, even if everything was addressed to her mother or her father. Clearly, the cousin was ready to believe that Candle was up to no good. If he sent Miss Bradshaw anything too personal, the cousin would be after him with one of those wheelwright's mallets Candle had seen at the workshop.

But flowers were very ordinary. He rather thought he was doing better than that.

Meanwhile, the news from Europe was bad. Napoleon had won a major battle, devastating the armies of the third coalition. From the reports in the newspaper, the allies had suffered devastating losses at a place called Ulm. Candle looked it up on the map in his study.

"Randall, dear." His mother's voice made him jump. Her new chair let her glide around the ground floor on her own. She loved the freedom it gave her, but he still wasn't used to her sudden appearances. Perhaps he should ask Miss Bradshaw if there was a way to make the wheels squeak.

"Mother," he said. He bent to kiss her check and examined her face as he did. She was too thin, too pale, and the pain lines around her eyes were highlighted by dark shadows from too many nights without sleep. "How are you, my dear?"

"Well, thank you, Randall," she said, as she always did.

"You haven't been sleeping. Won't you take the medicine the doctor gave you? Just for one night?"

"It gives me bad dreams, Randall, and makes my head feel as if it is stuffed with cotton wool. Now do not fuss, dear one. It is a mother's job to fret over her child, not the other way around. I came to ask if you would run some messages for me when you go into Bath."

"Willingly, of course. What do you need?"

"I have a list."

It came as no surprise that most of what Mother wanted was for her garden. She was so looking forward to the new outdoor chair so she could supervise the plantings of the new bulbs she wanted him to buy. Her favourite nursery company had sent her a catalogue with hand-tinted tulips and crocuses. "They will be so pretty next year, Randall."

"You'll be careful, won't you? You will stay indoors if the weather is unkind? You will wrap up warm?"

"You are fussing again, my son," she scolded.

"You're very precious to me, Mother. May I not look after you?"

"You need a wife of your own to fuss over, I think. What of this Miss Bradshaw who made the chairs?"

"Miss Bradshaw?" Sometimes, Candle thought, his mother lifted thoughts right out of people's heads. How else would she know to ask that question? Confined to a bed and now a chair, she didn't see him around the estate organising deliveries to Bath, and she didn't have access to his correspondence.

"Don't look surprised, dearest. I am your mother. I know you better than anyone on earth. Your eyes go soft and misty when you mention her, and you have mentioned her several times every day since you came home."

She frowned a little. "I do hope you have resolved whatever came between you last time."

"Last time." What did she know about last time?

"Lady Cresthover wrote to me when you began to show an interest in Miss Bradshaw at Lady Cresthover's house party. A charity case of her daughter's, she said, and perhaps not suitable for a peer's son. But Lady Cresthover is a silly woman, so I discounted that. And then she wrote again to say that you had broken the poor girl's heart by courting her for her money. Which is patently ridiculous, Randall, because you would never do such a thing."

"I hope you told her so, Mother."

"Oh no, Randall dearest. Such gossips are so useful when one does not go out in Society much. As long as one keeps in mind that 90% of what they say is exaggerated and the rest is invented. I would not discourage Lady Cresthover's letters for the world. So have you resolved your difficulties with Miss Bradshaw?"

"I am working on it, Mother. You wouldn't mind?"

"Mind you marrying into a trade family? Darling boy, I am from a merchant family, which the gentry consider to be the same thing. Except your father married me for my money, whereas you are in love, are you not?"

"I think so," Candle said. "I think I have loved her since I first met her."

Lord Avery must have left an order at the shop, because more flowers arrived the day after he left, and more the day after that. Then the first package arrived: an edition of Mother Goose Tales, Robert Sanders' translation of Charles Perrault's fairy tales. The story of the Little Glass Slipper was among them. It had clearly been much read.

"Who is it from," Mama asked.

"There is no note," Min told her, but she had no doubt who had sent the package.

The flowers kept arriving, different each day. The miscellaneous baskets of the first day gave way to blue salvia and tea roses the second, wrapped in ivy and ferns. The ivy and ferns reappeared on the third day with zinnia flowers, and on the fourth—the day the book arrived—irises.

The bouquet of white roses and daisies on the fifth day had the usual ivy and ferns, but sprigs of myrtle and rosemary had been added, and after that, the flowers changed every day but they always came with ivy, ferns, myrtle, and rosemary.

On the sixth day, two brace of pheasants, a basket of apples, and a large bag of walnuts were delivered to the kitchen, this time with a note to Min's mother. "Viscount Avery begs that Mrs Bradshaw will accept this small offering from his estate."

Mama raised her eyebrows, but said nothing. That day, the flowers were delicate orchids, and the following brought anemones.

On the next day, she was hovering in the hall when the yellow roses arrived.

"More flowers from your young man, Minerva?" It was Mama, watching her from the stairs.

Minerva, sure her smile was beyond fatuous, pretended to sniff the roses until she could school her face to calm again.

"He is not mine, Mama. He is just amusing himself, as the aristocracy do."

She hurried away before Mama could say more. The skins had arrived at the workshop the previous evening, and she had a chair to cover.

The ninth day brought hollyhocks and a jug of cider addressed to Papa, prompting Papa to ask what "young Avery is after, trying to turn me up sweet."

"Minnie, Uncle George," Daniel explained. "Lord Avery is after Minnie."

"I can see that," Papa growled, "but what does he mean by it, that's what I want to know."

"He means to court her, George," Mama said. "That's what the myrtle means. Myrtle for marriage, ivy for faithfulness, ferns for sincerity, and rosemary for remembrance."

Min had taken four days to realise that Lord Avery's choices were deliberate, and had been able to decipher only some of the messages. Mama might have said she knew what they meant!

"He sent blue salvia and tea roses first; that's 'you occupy my thoughts, always'. Then zinnias for absent friends; 'I miss you.' The day after that, he sent irises; 'your friendship means so much to me'. He sent white roses and daisies on the day he added the myrtle and rosemary. White roses and daisies are both for innocence. 'I remember you are an innocent, and I intend marriage.' He followed those with anemones, which mean fragile or forsaken. With the myrtle and the rest, he means, 'My heart is fragile; do not forsake me.' Orchids for beauty the next day; 'I find you beautiful'. Then yellow roses for friendship and caring; 'I care for you and wish to have your friendship.' Today's blossom is hollyhock. That means ambition; 'I strive to win you'."

Daniel and Papa stared at Mama, and then turned to contemplate Min.

"I had better put these in water," Min said, wanting time on her own to think about what Mama had said. Did Lord Avery really mean all of that?

But even if he did, he was still a peer, and the gap between them was still too large.

Now that Mother had opened the way, Candle found himself talking to her about Miss Bradshaw. He'd never told anyone about the ill-fated house party, but he could make a story of it without bitterness now that he knew that he and his beloved had been the victims of malicious scheming.

"Why would they do it, Mother?" he wondered.

"I can think of a number of reasons, Randall. Some people like to break anything pretty or pleasing. They cannot stand for other people to be happy. From what you say, the brother thought of you as his natural victim. And the sister probably felt the same about Miss Bradshaw. I daresay the pair of you ignored them, and they would hate that."

Candle nodded. "I wouldn't even remember them being there if Miss Kitteridge had not been the one to tell me Miss Bradshaw was gone."

"Another possibility is that Miss Kitteridge had hopes of her own. It was about that time my brother retired to England, and she may have thought you would inherit— which you did, of course, though not until this year."

"I don't think so, she wasn't even nice to me... although..." Candle stared into the past for a moment. "Actually, around six months later she tried to... warm the acquaintance, I suppose. All of a sudden, she seemed to be at all the events I went to, and she stopped making cutting remarks and—I got the impression she wanted me as part of her court."

"I expect she hadn't been in town till then."

Candle agreed. Kitteridge and his sister had come up to London for the Season.

"So what did you do," Mother asked.

Candle flushed a little. "Seeing her reminded me of losing Miss Bradshaw. So I stopped going into Society until she left London again."

"And then look what she did next."

"I don't know what she did next."

"She married Baron Norton, Randall dear. And gave birth to a very premature baby five months after the wedding. A son, after Lord Norton's previous four wives had failed to have any children at all."

"Good Heavens, Mother. Are you suggesting what I think you are suggesting?"

"I think you were Miss Kitteridge's first choice to father her cuckoo. On the whole, she did not do too badly in choosing Lord Norton."

"You shock me, Mother. You think him a preferable husband to me?"

"I think she would have found you far less malleable than she expected. And Lord Norton suffered a seizure at the christening party after over-imbibing in celebratory punch. He was dead before his heir was six months old. Yes, she didn't do too badly at all. Of course, the money is in trust for the little heir, and she is not a trustee. Or the boy's guardian. But Lord Norton left her a moderate income and a house in Bath as her widow's portion."

"How on earth do you know all this, Mother."

Mother smiled, gently. "I told you Lady Cresthover has her uses."

Sunday morning brought carnations, a mixed bunch of red and white. "'You are sweet and lovely, and my heart aches for you'," Mama translated.

After the Sunday service, Daniel found Min in the conservatory, sketching an improvement to the gearing that moved the wheels on a merlin chair.

"What's that you've got? Something for one of your chairs?" he asked.

"A gearing," she said, shortly, but he didn't take the hint.

"I'm glad I found you alone. Are Uncle George and Aunt Gavriella..." he looked around as if he was expecting them to leap out from behind one of the potted ferns.

"Papa is resting, and Mama is sitting with him."

Daniel looked alarmed, and Min hastened to reassure him. "He is just tired. You have been working long hours, and he is not a young man."

"Yes. It has been hard on him, but you know how he is. He needs to watch over everything." Daniel shook his head. "I've told him he needs to slow down. But he won't."

"He will soon. He says he plans to retire once this contract is signed. When do you expect that?"

"We'll have the order done tomorrow, so that will be the worst of it. We won't be able to relax till the client has finished inspections, but by the end of the week we'll know for certain whether the contract is going ahead." Daniel grimaced. "I don't know, though. He has talked about retirement before, but it has never happened."

"Mama has never been in favour before," Min told him. "This time, she is saying it is time to let go. She knows you can handle it. I know you can handle it. Even Papa knows. You are an excellent manager, and of course it will all be yours one day."

She had resented that, when she was younger; being overlooked as an heir to the carriage works just because she was female. But building the chair business had taught her her father's decision to choose Daniel to inherit was a practical one. The buyers wanted to deal with a man. The suppliers wanted to deal with a man. The workers wanted to deal with a man. At every turn, she had to prove herself, struggle against their preconceptions, and—even then—often call her father or her cousin to back her up.

She was slowly building a reputation and a set of relationships that made those help calls less necessary, but her father's support meant she remained in business while she did so.

"Thank you, Minnie. That means a lot to me, to have you say that."

"So what did you want to say to me, Daniel?"

Uncharacteristically, Daniel looked at his feet. "Minnie, I was wondering, are you going to accept Lord Avery?"

No, she wasn't, but she choked on saying so. "He has not asked me, Daniel."

"Aunt Gavriella says he will. She is generally right, you know."

"It would not work, Daniel, you know that. They can put up with us if we stay in our place, the upper classes. But if we dare to think we are as good as they are…" She trailed off. Daniel had been to a school for gentlemen. He knew how the gentry treated their sort.

"Perhaps. Well, what about Billingham?"

"Are you trying to marry me off, Daniel?"

"Minnie, you have to see. If your father retires and moves away, you can't stay here. You can't go on working in the yard, and you can't go on living in the same house as me. There. That's what I came to say."

His back was stiff with embarrassment as he left.

Min sat by herself for a long time. Of course she couldn't stay. Cousins though they were, and raised as brother and sister, they could not live under the one roof without Mama and Papa in the house.

As soon as Daniel said so, she realised it. Mama and Papa planned to retire to a country village where Mama could have a garden and, Papa said, where Daniel wouldn't feel Papa breathing down his neck.

But she hadn't considered how that might affect her. How foolish.

When the last of the order was filled the next day, Papa took the rest of the afternoon off.

"Papa, may I walk with you?" Min asked.

"Leaving early, daughter?" Papa said. "Yes, walk with me." He offered her his arm, and they set off down the road together. "I want to ask you about Lord Avery," Papa said. "Roses, this morning, was it? What does Mama say about that?"

"Buds of moss roses with lily of the valley. 'Confessions of love to one who is sweet', Mama said." She mightn't want Lord Avery's pursuit, but she couldn't help be touched.

"Do you like him, daughter?"

"It does not matter, Papa. He is a viscount, and I am a carriage-maker's daughter. It would not work."

"Is he a good man, Little Owl?" Papa hadn't called her 'Little Owl' in years. It was his pet name for her, a reference to the familiar of the goddess she was named for.

"I think he is, Papa. But he is still a viscount. Papa, have you thought about where you and Mama will go when you retire?"

"I have promised Mama a garden. I have promised Daniel that I won't look over his shoulder. And I've promised myself I'll be close enough to Bath to come back if Daniel needs me." Papa laughed at his own reluctance to let go.

"Anywhere in particular, Papa?"

Papa shook his head. "We haven't started looking, yet. After Christmas. After Christmas we will decide a place and a date. Do you have a place you would like, daughter?"

"I do not mind, Papa. As long as it has a workshop big enough for me to make my chairs."

"You should be making babies, not chairs," Papa grumbled. "Marry your viscount or choose another man, and give me and Mama grand-babies."

"I would marry a man who would let me make my chairs," Min said.

"Ah Min. Your Mama was right. She told me that if I encouraged you I would end up breaking your heart. Min. Little Owl. Face facts. Women aren't meant to make carriages, even your little ones. I've let you make your chairs and sell them, and a very good job you have done of it too.

I've been very proud of you. But a man doesn't want his wife to go out to work."

"You let Mama work in the harness shop," Min protested.

"Remember that, do you? I had no choice, Min. We didn't have the money, when we started out, to hire a good harness maker. Mama was the best. But as soon as I could, I replaced her so she could stay home. A man doesn't want his wife to go out to work. Looking after the home, visiting her friends. That's enough."

Not for me, Min wanted to say, but Papa kept talking.

"No, Min, give up this notion and look around for a husband. I don't blame you for not wanting Billingham. How a bright man like his father has such a foolish son is beyond me. But come out of your workshop sometimes. Go to a few dinners and parties. Meet people. Look around. What do you say, Min? It'll be fun."

Chapter five: News from abroad

Candle arrived in Bath on the evening of the 6th, and had to fight the urge to go immediately in search of Miss Bradshaw. He wandered down to the florist shop. Mrs Brown, the florist, greeted him with enthusiasm.

"Have the deliveries gone as planned?" he asked, and was assured that flowers had been delivered every morning. He and Mrs Brown had spent nearly two hours, the week before last, planning the flowers to send and the order to send them.

"My delivery boy tells me that the whole household waits each morning to see what's next," Mrs Brown said. "It's the Christmas Roses for tomorrow, sir?"

Candle nodded. 'I am all anxiety until I see you,' they meant. The large pot of honey from the estate's hives should have been delivered this morning. He had sent a note presenting his compliments to Mr Bradshaw, and asking leave to call on him tomorrow afternoon. Half his anxiety was for what Mr Bradshaw might say, and the rest for his beloved. Had his persistent assault by flower and food softened her towards him? He could only hope so.

He made his way back to the White Hart Inn, surprised at the number of people on the streets. His friend Michaels was in the crowd in front of the inn.

"There's been a great battle," he told Candle, not bothering with greetings. "Someone who's come in on the coach is going to read the Gazette. They're just setting him up in a window so everyone can hear."

"Where? A battle where?" Candle was torn between staying to listen and rushing across the river to assure himself of Miss Bradshaw's safety.

"A sea battle. A victory, they say, but Nelson is dead."

The great Nelson, dead. It was hard to believe.

"Is it true?" Candle turned at the new voice. Miss Bradshaw's cousin, with a much older man. "Is Nelson dead?"

"So I'm told, Mr Whitlow." Candle introduced Whitlow and Michaels, and was in turn introduced to the older man, Mr Bradshaw. He was built on the same powerful lines as his nephew, but had eyes as grey as his daughter's.

"So you're Lord Avery," he said.

"Quiet," Michaels interrupted. "He's starting."

From an open window on the second floor of the inn, a stout man in a florid waistcoat began, "Dispatches, of which the following are Copies, were received at the Admiralty this day, at one o'clock a.m., from Vice-Admiral Collingwood, Commander in Chief of his Majesty's ships and vessels of Cadiz."

At the words 'Commander in Chief', a murmur ran through the crowd, followed by whispered commands to hush.

"Euryalus, off Cape Trafalgar. October 22nd, 1805," the reader continued.

He paused, and looked out at the people, silent below him.

"Sir,— The ever-to-be-lamented death of Vice-Admiral, Lord Viscount Nelson, who in the late conflict with the enemy fell in the hour of victory, leaves to me the duty..."

The crowd listened for the most part in hushed silence, though they cheered when the reader reported, "...it pleased the Almighty Disposer of all events to grant His Majesty's arms a complete and glorious victory," and groaned at, "His Lordship received a musket ball in his left breast... and soon after expired."

It took nearly 40 minutes to read the two closely printed sides of the newsheet. Afterwards, the crowd dispersed in small clumps, all discussing the news.

"I don't know whether to cheer or weep," Candle said.

"I know, lad," Mr Bradshaw agreed. "Napoleon has suffered a heavy loss, that's certain. But Nelson is a heavy loss to our dear England."

Michaels muttered something about an appointment and left. Candle didn't fancy going into the inn. The noisy public bar or a lonely private room—neither appealed. For want of a better option, he walked with Mr Bradshaw and Whitlow around the Roman Baths and past the Abbey towards the bridge.

"So you're the young lord who has turned my house into a flower shop and who wants to come and see me tomorrow," Mr Bradshaw said.

No time like the present. "Yes, Sir. I wish to ask your permission to court your daughter, Sir."

"You're already courting my daughter, seemingly. Unless you are carrying on a clandestine affair with my dear wife." Mr Bradshaw looked stern, but one of Candle's colonels had displayed just such a twinkle when apparently chewing out a subordinate he was pleased with.

"After all, Uncle, he has sent Aunt Gavrielle all those flowers and most of the notes," Whitlow offered, finding his own remark enormously amusing.

"You'd better come to dinner, then," Mr Bradshaw said, and led the way onto the bridge. "Do you think this victory will stop the Corsican?"

"It will at least stop him from invading England until he has built some more ships," Candle said.

"Yes," Whitlow agreed. "We don't know the details yet, but whatever ships we've lost will be replaced by the ships we've captured from the French and the Spanish."

"Nothing will make up for the loss of Nelson," Mr Bradshaw said.

Candle nodded, but was still thinking about stopping Napoleon. "We can hold Napoleon off by sea, but we'll need to meet him on land to end his ambitions."

They continued discussing the battle and its implications for the rest of the walk, until Mr Bradshaw opened his front door and ushered Candle inside.

Miss Bradshaw and a much older woman, clearly related, were just descending the stairs.

"My love," Mr Bradshaw told his wife, "I have brought Lord Avery for dinner, and we have sad but glorious news."

It was Lord Avery. Here. In her house. She had been steeling herself to be indifferent to him tomorrow, when he came for the chair. Now was too early. She wasn't ready.

He smiled at her, and her knees turned to jelly. Yesterday he'd sent asters ('I love you'), a watercolour of a country house, and a note that said his mother had asked him to send her mother a painting she'd made of their home, Avery Hall.

This morning, it had been damask roses and stephanotis, plus a large pot of honey. The flowers, Mama said, meant 'I send these flowers as an ambassador of my love, and I look to be happy in marriage'. The note that asked for an interview with Papa needed no interpreter.

And now he was here. In her house. Almost a whole day early.

Something they were saying caught her ear; something about Nelson?

"Dead?" Mama was asking.

"Just a moment," Papa said. He turned to the butler. "Heath, assemble the staff in the drawing room. They'll want to hear this."

Min took a seat with Mama in the drawing room, and—once the house's servants were gathered—listened to the report of the battle, the great victory, and the great loss.

Lord Avery stayed with the two women after the staff had dispersed and Papa and Daniel had gone upstairs to change for dinner.

"Will this loss of all his navy stop Napoleon, do you think?" Mama asked.

"It will stop him invading us, Ma'am," Candle answered, "at least for the moment. It won't stop him rampaging all over the continent."

Mama had more questions, and Min was content to sit and watch Mama and Lord Avery talk. The other two joined them and they all went in to a much delayed dinner.

Napoleon and Nelson continued to dominate the conversation. Lord Avery was knowledgeable and ready to defend his own opinion, but also willing to change his mind if someone else offered a persuasive argument. And he showed no signs of distinguishing between the arguments of the women and those of the men; none of the condescension Min was used to from every man she knew. Even Papa and Daniel were not quite exceptions, since she was sure they'd just learned to keep their condescension veiled from her and Mama.

By the second setting, Min had forgotten her wariness. Lord Avery behaved as if he came to dinner every day, and the family all treated him as if he belonged.

"Cook used your honey in this, lad," Papa told him, taking a spoonful of the syllabub.

"It is good, isn't it," Lord Avery replied. "My beekeeper tells me that this year's honey is particularly strong in orchard flavours. The fruit trees blossomed well, I'm told."

Mama's eyes crinkled at the corners, as she smiled at Lord Avery. "I have not thanked you, yet, for all the lovely flowers you sent me. Such charming messages."

He took her teasing in his stride. "A fitting tribute to your beauty, Mrs Bradshaw."

After dinner, Min reluctantly left the dining room with Mama. What would Papa and Daniel say to Lord Avery with the women out of the room? What would he say to them?

"I like your Lord Avery, child," Mama said, breaking into her thoughts. "But he is still an aristocrat, however nice he may be."

"He is not mine, Mama. I am not foolish enough to think I could marry a peer."

"I worry, my love. I do not want to see you hurt. And I cannot help but remember what happened when we sent you to school."

"So, Lord Avery," Mr Bradshaw began, as soon as the door shut behind the two women. "You want permission to court my daughter."

Candle hadn't thought to have this conversation in front of a witness, but if that was the way Mr Bradshaw wanted it, so be it.

Mr Bradshaw correctly interpreted his glance at Whitlow. "Daniel is Minerva's cousin and my heir. If anything happens to me, you'll be dealing with him."

Candle nodded in acknowledgement. "Yes, Sir. I want permission to court your daughter."

"Rumour has it that you're a warm man, thanks to your uncle. Think you can keep it?"

"Yes, Sir. I think I can. I'm not a man of profligate habits, and I'm working hard to learn the estate my father left me and the business my uncle left me. I mean to make a success of them both."

It was Mr Bradshaw's turn to nod. "So I'm told." To Candle's surprised look, he said, "I asked questions, lad. She's my one ewe lamb. Of course I asked questions."

"I understand." Little though Candle liked the idea of someone poking around and asking about him, he did understand Mr Bradshaw's need to protect his daughter. "And were you content with the answers, Sir?"

Mr Bradshaw didn't answer him directly. "She says she won't have you. She says that the middle sort and the peerage don't mix, and that a marriage between you won't work. What do you say to that?"

"I hope to change her mind," Candle said. "I think we can make it work. Yes, the Society cats will have their claws out, but we don't need to live in Society. And my mother and I will love her just as she is."

"Love, is it? You said so with your flowers. Do you say it straight, lad? To me, and to Daniel here?"

Candle met his eyes and said, firmly, "I love her. I love your daughter, Sir."

"Well, Daniel?" Mr Bradshaw asked.

"I'd say give him your blessing, Uncle, and wish him luck. She's stubborn, my cousin. You'll find you need all the luck you can get."

"My blessing? No. No offense, lad, but I'll save my blessing for my lass if she decides to accept you. She'll need it, and a powerful load of luck. Mixing your sort and mine; I've seen a lot of sorrow come that way. But I won't deny my Minerva if you're the one she wants. You can court her, Lord Avery. But as to where the luck lies..."

Mr Bradford shook his head and poured them all another glass of port.

Candle exerted himself to be agreeable, and by the time they joined the ladies, Candle and Daniel Whitlow were on first-name terms.

Miss Bradshaw was at a desk in the corner, and Mrs Bradshaw sat sewing by the fire. Her tambour was half filled with colourful flowers, bursting joyously across the canvas.

Candle stopped to admire the embroidery, then looked over Miss Bradshaw's shoulder. Engineering designs. He might have known.

"It's gearing of some kind," he said.

She went to put her work away. "No, don't let me stop you working," he said. "But would you explain it to me?"

An hour later when he took his leave, he was much more knowledgeable about the benefits of differential gearing. He'd found it strangely compelling—Miss Bradshaw was experimenting with progressive changes in size so that less strength was needed to work the mechanism, while still keeping the mechanism light enough and small enough not to weigh down the chair.

They'd agreed he would come to the works in the morning. Candle was keen to get home to Avery Hall with the news of the battle, and he'd leave the White Hart as soon as the morning mail coach arrived with the newspapers from London.

"I'll bring copies for you, Sir," he told Mr Bradshaw.

Crossing the foyer of the hotel, he was hailed by a peremptory, "Lord Avery!"

He turned to see a dumpling of a woman whose generous figure was amplified by a plethora of floating scarves, fringes and ruffles in shades of purple. Lady Cresthover. She was bearing down on him, her daughter and Lady Norton in her wake. For a fleeting moment he contemplated pretending not to hear and bolting for the stairs. He resisted the temptation. The old besom was his mother's friend. Sort of.

He pasted on his best social smile, and gave each lady a small bow. "Lady Cresthover. Miss Cresthover. Lady Norton."

"Lord Avery, what brings you to Bath? How is your dear mother? And what do you think of this terrible news about Nelson? Do you think Napoleon is finished, as they are saying? How long are you in Bath?"

The questions came in quick succession, while Lady Cresthover took him by the arm and herded him into a private parlour.

"The girls and I are just about to have supper. You will join us, Lord Avery." This was a royal command, not a question. When Candle protested that he had already eaten, he was bidden to sit and have a glass of wine, and to answer Lady Cresthover's questions.

An experienced officer of His Majesty's Coldstream Guard should show courage under fire. Besides, he was considerably taller than he'd been twelve years ago; last time Lady Cresthover had rapped him on the head with her formidable thimble. She would have trouble reaching his head now.

"Certainly, my Lady," he said. "Could you repeat them one at a time, please?"

It was an hour before he was finally able to make his excuses, citing the trip he needed to take the following morning. By then, he'd drawn several conclusions.

Lady Cresthover's incessant gossip, though often ill-informed, was not ill-intended, but Lady Norton was a cat of quite a different colour. Lady Norton had her knife out for Miss Bradshaw—she had made several derogatory comments, which Candle judged it best to ignore or deflect, since any defence would just encourage the lady to make trouble.

Lady Cresthover, on the other hand, proclaimed Miss Bradshaw, 'a sweet girl, quite the lady, and a very good friend to poor Nelly Maybury, when her husband died'.

And Miss Cresthover also came to Miss Bradshaw's defence, insisting that Miss Bradshaw was far more of a lady 'than some who lay claim to the term'.

Lady Cresthover and her daughter might be allies if the new Viscountess Avery wanted to go into Society.

Oh yes, and he'd learned one more thing. Lady Norton's schoolgirl nickname of Kitty Cat was an insult to felines everywhere.

Lord Avery collected the chair and was gone from Bath by 11 o'clock in the morning. Min found the rest of the day sadly flat. He hadn't said anything lover-like as the chair was tied to the back of his carriage, but the warmth in his eyes had set her tingling.

Perhaps she only imagined it. Perhaps, too, she imagined the press of his fingers when he said, as he took his farewell, "I very much look forward to seeing you and your mother in three weeks, Miss Bradshaw."

That morning's floral tribute spoke of anxiety. If he felt anxiety, he didn't show it. She was the one who was anxious, her heartbeat speeding up when she thought of him, the heat igniting in her belly at the mere thought of the warmth in his eyes.

She was the one who couldn't keep her mind on her work, who had lost interest in food, who lay awake at night remembering every gesture, every word, every look.

She would not fall in love with a peer. She could not. She was not so foolish. Was she?

Chapter six: A visit to the country

The flowers kept coming, the type repeated, but in different combinations each day. Each day, Mama interpreted the message for her, and Daniel took great delight in offering an alternative reading. According to Mama, Christmas roses and asters with sprays of mimosa meant 'My concealed love is now disclosed. How will it be received?' Daniel suggested, 'I wish to hide because the thought of love makes me anxious.' Blue salvia, irises and yellow roses meant 'I think of you, miss you, and long for your friendship' to Mama. But Daniel claimed it meant 'When I think of you, I miss having friends'.

The gifts of produce from the estate kept coming too, prompting Cook to tell Daniel (who passed it on to Min) that she hoped Miss wouldn't turn the young Lord down too soon, because his presents were so useful.

Walking home from the workshop one afternoon, Polly in attendance, Min had to stop suddenly to avoid a fashionably-dressed young woman who burst out of a shop door without looking, to stand frozen in the road, her hands clenched at her sides and her face stiff with the effort of holding back tears.

Min, who had been about to circle around her, took a second look. "Cara? What's wrong? May I help?"

Caroline Cresthover had been closer to a friend than any of the other girls at the select girl's seminary Min's parents had sent her to.

"Min? Min Bradshaw? Oh Min, if I had stayed in the shop I would have killed that woman." The tears had escaped, spilling down Cara's cheeks.

The shop door opened to let out a maid carrying a reticule that matched Cara's pelisse. Min could see past her to Lady Norton and a gaggle of her friends. Kitty Cat was clearly up to her usual tricks.

"Do not let her see that she upsets you," Min counselled Cara. "Come; let us move away where they cannot see us."

"I know I should be charitable, but..."

"Never mind being charitable. Just do not give her a stick to beat you with." Min turned to the maid. "Do you have a handkerchief for your mistress? Here, Cara, dry your tears and let's go and have tea and tear Kitty Cat's character to tiny little shreds."

Over tea, Cara confided that Vivi Norton loved to commiserate with her about being 'on the shelf', which Cara mostly ignored. But today's nasty remarks had included a series of snippets about the activities of one Captain Marsh who, according to Lady Norton, had cut a swathe through the widows of London and was about to announce his engagement to a debutante of 17.

"And Vivi says she is blonde and slender, and everyone knows that slender blondes are more fashionable." Cara, whose hair and eyes were brown, and who was generously curved, began to cry again.

"Captain Marsh is special to you?" Min ventured. It seemed a safe enough guess.

"He said we would announce our engagement as soon as he had the approval of his grandfather. His father is the third son of the Earl of Scuncester. He said we had to keep our courtship secret in case his grandfather did not approve."

"If it was a secret, Cara, how did Vivi find out?"

Cara blushed. "I might have hinted. Just a little. Only in the strictest confidence, and only because she teased me so about being twenty and unmarried."

Several cream cakes cheered Cara up. She was not, Min deduced, particularly attached to Captain Marsh. His status as the grandson of an Earl and his professed interest in marrying her seemed to be the sum total of his attractive features. Cara found his conversation boring, his lack of dancing skill annoying, and his repeated attempts to kiss her frightening.

"Mama said I should never be alone with a man because he would try to kiss me, and then I would be ruined," she told Min. "I wasn't even alone with Captain Marsh; well, not really alone. The first time was in the garden, and there were other people there, but it was dark and we couldn't see them. And Mama was right. He did try to kiss me. I did not let him, though." She nodded, pleased with herself.

"And then the next week he stopped me in the hall at a party. He said he was dying of love for me, which was very romantic, I thought. And he asked me to meet him outside and tried to kiss me again when I said no. I told him I did not want to be ruined. He said I would not be ruined for just one kiss. That was when he said he planned to marry me. He said it was alright to kiss the man you were going to marry. But Mama came and he went away."

"Then what happened?" Min was finding the whole saga morbidly fascinating.

"He kept trying to get me on my own so he could kiss me. And in the end, I let him. It was not very nice." Cara frowned. "It was wet. And I could not breathe properly. Has anyone kissed you, Min?"

Min shook her head, mostly to dislodge a sudden wish to know how nice Lord Avery's kiss might be. Certainly she had, on several occasions, seen Mama and Papa kiss, and Mama seemed to like it very well.

"I do not recommend it," Cara said.

"Perhaps Captain Marsh is not very good at it," Min suggested.

Cara shrugged. "Anyway, then he went off to London. He said that he could not write because we could not yet announce our betrothal, but that I should just wait and he would come back. He did not mean it, did he Min?"

"I do not think so, from what you have told me, Cara."

"Well, I do not care. But I would have liked to have one over that cat Vivi. You know that she had to marry? She would have been ruined if she did not, my Mama says. But now she is Baroness Norton and she takes precedence over me, and it is just not fair, Min."

Cara helped herself to another cream cake, which seemed to console her.

"Vivi is not very popular you know, Min. I only spend time with her because she is my cousin. Most of the girls we were at school with do not like her at all." This seemed to console Cara even more. "I know, come to my afternoon at home tomorrow. The girls would be so pleased to see you."

Min refused, but Cara was so enthusiastic about the idea that, in the end, she went. To her surprise, she enjoyed herself, and even accepted an invitation to walk in the Sydney Gardens with a group of the ladies later that week.

It seemed that most of them had suffered under the rule of Vivi Kitteridge's little group. Min, sunk in her own misery, had never realised that the school was split into two groups. On the one side, the vast majority, trying hard not to be noticed. On the other, Kitty Cat and her three disciples.

But outside of the enclosed environment of the school, the small group of bullies had lost their power. Even Cara, most of the time, ignored Lady Norton's spitefulness, though she couldn't completely cut herself off from her cousin.

"Randall, darling, do stop pacing. You have been to the window so many times the carpet is developing a groove." Mother was smiling. His nervousness amused her. How nice for Mother.

"I wish they had let me escort them," Candle said. Had he met them in Bath, they would be here by now, or—at the very least—he would know the delay was because they had left Bath late, and not because of any of the disasters along the way he could picture all too clearly.

"Do you think she'll like her room," he asked.

"Randall, you have asked me the same question three times in the last hour. And driven Mrs Howard nearly demented in changing Miss Bradshaw's room six times in as many days, moving furniture in and then out again, and I do not know what else. I know you want everything to be perfect, my love, but just relax. I'm sure your Miss Bradshaw will like her room."

"My Lord." It was the butler. "Young Jem has just arrived my Lord." Jem was the youngest groom, and had been posted on a hill overlooking the road from Bath, as an early warning system.

"They're coming?"

"Yes, my Lord. A chaise, my Lord, coming fast."

Not too fast, he hoped. That bend at the bottom of the hill could be tricky at speed. He should have had the curve reformed in the summer.

"Whatever you are worrying about now, Randall, don't," Mother said.

The chaise arrived safely at the foot of the stairs, and Candle was at the door with an umbrella almost before it had come to a stop. Daniel descended first, but stepped under the umbrella a footman offered him and waved to invite Candle to hand down first Mrs Bradshaw, then her daughter, and then the maid, Polly.

He handed Mrs Bradshaw over to Daniel and escorted Miss Bradshaw inside himself, leaving the footman with a third umbrella to bring the maid in.

Daniel wouldn't stay, saying that he needed to get back to Bath. After a cup of tea and a plate of sandwiches, he took leave of his aunt and cousin.

"I'll be back for you in four days," he told them, then met Candle's eyes over their heads. "You'll take care of my family,

Candle," he said; a statement, not a question. Candle agreed, anyway.

Mrs Bradshaw went to rest to recover from the trip. Miss Bradshaw refused the suggestion, and instead closeted herself with Mother to ask questions about the chair. At a loose end, Candle took himself off to his study, but he couldn't settle to work. Not with her in the house at last.

He wanted to show her everything. He wanted to hold her and kiss her till she agreed to stay forever. No. That would frighten her off. But somehow he would find a way to convince her that she belonged with him. She was only here for a few days. He would have to make the most of them.

Lord Avery's mother was a darling. She never complained, though she was clearly often in pain. Instead, she would turn the conversation somewhere else. Min coaxed her into being clear about how the chairs worked for her.

"If anything hurts or is uncomfortable, I want to know so that I can fix it, my Lady."

Afterwards, Min went in search of Lord Avery. The butler directed her to the study, where he was working at a huge old desk, his back to the large window. The fitful rain of the past few days had cleared, and sunlight was pouring over Lord Avery's shoulder onto his work. The light glanced off his red hair, setting gleaming threads on fire.

He felt her gaze and looked up, meeting her eyes with a slowly warming smile that set light to a slow burn in her.

"Miss Bradshaw, please come in."

"I am sorry to disturb your work, Lord Avery."

He rounded the desk and set a chair for her, hovering over her as if he wanted to guide her physically into the seat. Her skin seemed to yearn towards him. She held herself stiffly in check.

"It is about your mother."

Lord Avery's eyes grew concerned, the heat that disturbed her banked for the moment.

"Is there something wrong?"

She hastened to reassure him. "Nothing we cannot fix. She is developing sore patches. Because she is unable to move herself, and because she has no feeling in her lower torso," Min blushed at mentioning such a word to a man. But it needed to be said.

Lord Avery frowned. "I will have a word with her maid. She must be more vigilant. Could we find an unguent or something to soothe...? But you said you could fix it. What is your plan, Miss Bradshaw?"

"What you suggest is good, and I have discussed it with your mother and the maid. But I would like to try something that one of my customers told me about. Would you be able to procure a sheepskin with the wool still on?"

"We keep sheep on the home farm, as well as up on the wolds. I should think I already own any number of sheepskins."

"Sitting on sheepskin may help. And lying on it, as well, in bed."

They talked a little more about the possible benefits, and Lord Avery sent a servant down to the home farm to order at least three skins of various depths and sizes.

"May I show you through the house, Miss Bradshaw?" he asked.

Min panicked. The thought of being alone with him, even in a house full of servants, suddenly seemed overwhelming. She muttered something about resting, and made her escape.

By dinner time, she was ashamed of herself. Lady Avery and Mama had discovered a mutual love of embroidery, and of the language of flowers. When Mama mentioned her hope of soon having a garden, this spread into a deep conversation about methods of cultivation, and what did best in their local climate. Lord Avery suggested a stroll in the picture gallery. Mama waved her compliance without halting what she was saying to Lady Avery. Min took Lord Avery's arm and let him conduct her down the hall.

The gallery stretched across the back of the house. He left her in the doorway while he lit candles in sconces all along the walls, then came back with a candelabra to escort her to the first picture.

The Averys had been at Avery Hall since the dawn of time, it seemed. And all had been recorded in paint for this moment; to look down in scorn and judgement on an interloper of the middle sort who had begun to dream of stepping out of her class.

Lord Avery took them in his stride, telling stories about the people in each portrait, describing them with affection and familiarity. He could, of course. He belonged here.

She nodded, and smiled, going through the motions from behind the wall she'd long since learned to erect. Never before with Lord Avery, though.

Suddenly, two thirds of the way down the long room, he stopped and turned her towards him, his hands on her shoulders.

"This was a stupid idea, wasn't it?" he said. "Look, Miss Bradshaw. Min." He released one shoulder to raise her chin with his finger, so that her eyes looked straight into his. "Min," he repeated, his voice pleading, "they don't matter. You have as many ancestors as I do, you know. All human beings do. But none of them matter, on either side. You matter. We matter. Don't let them come between us."

Lost in his eyes, she couldn't remember why they should. There was only him. Randall. Ran.

He stooped, curling his head down to her height and brushing her lips gently with his. A soft caress of the lips, over too quickly.

She gave a small sound of distress, quickly stifled. He was right to stop. They were alone, unchaperoned. Mama trusted her to behave.

As if he could read her mind, he said, "We had better go back, Min. Your Mama trusts me, and I'm afraid I cannot be trusted too far. I should not be alone with you. Will you...?" He didn't finish his sentence, but just gestured to the door at the far end of the gallery.

She led the way, silently. Her knees did not quite belong to her; she felt as if she needed to carefully plan each step in advance or she would find herself in another room, another house.

As she approached the door, a painting on the other side caught her eye—a man on a horse with the look of Ran. He was older though, and the artist had caught a mood, an expression that she'd never seen on Ran's face. This man's face, Min thought, would fall easily into a sneer or a leer, but never into the kindness that was natural to his son. She didn't need Ran's muttered: "My father, the previous Viscount Avery," to tell the relationship.

Somehow, her earlier discomfort with the array of ancestors had gone, but Ran was tense and miserable beside her. "He was not a good man," she said, afraid when she heard her voice that she'd gone too far.

But Ran nodded. "You're right. He was an indifferent landlord, a neglectful father, and a bad husband. He wasn't a bad man, exactly. He just never grew up."

"A lot of Society men are like that," Min said.

"Yes. When we are children, we think our parents are unique. But he was very ordinary, really."

"He made you unhappy."

"He ignored me, mostly. He spent all of his time in London, and I stayed here at Avery Hall with Mother. I had a wonderful childhood. Then Father took it into his head that he should send me away to school."

She was holding his hand. She wasn't sure how that happened, but she squeezed it. She didn't need to be told that he hated school. Min had been miserable enough as a day pupil. Ran went to Eton, far away from home.

Again, his thoughts had tracked hers. "I lived for the holidays when I could come home."

"Your mother must have missed you."

From his surprised look, he hadn't considered that. "Yes. She was always so calm, I had not thought... But, yes. Poor Mother. I never really came back. Just holidays. I went from school to Oxford, to the Guard."

He looked so sad. She put her arms around him to give him a hug, and his came around her. With her head on his chest, she could hear his heart thumping. He shifted, so his body moved back from hers, and she blushed. How forward he must think her.

One moment Candle had been lost in a sad past, and the next he could think of nothing but the woman in his arms. He'd had to move her away from his groin. He wasn't sure how much Min knew about male anatomy. He'd like nothing better than to teach her, preferably right this minute, what the hardness he was hiding from her was for. No. He had enough sense left to know that he shouldn't take the power of choice away from her.

"Min? We need to go back to our mothers."

She had turned the most delightful pink. He wondered how far it spread then shut that thought off. It was not helping.

"I apologise, Lord..."

"Ssshh." He put a finger on her lips to stop her. "No apologies. I won't apologise to you for desiring you, and you won't apologise for being kind when I needed kindness. And it certainly isn't my fault or yours that you are still my goddess."

She smiled against his finger and he couldn't resist tracing the smile. One day; one day soon, he would feast on those generous lips.

Min asked questions, took measurements, made adjustments, and asked more questions. But by the end of the second day of her visit, she had run out of things she could do unless the rain let up for long enough to take the chair out of doors.

Everywhere she looked, Avery Hall showed signs of coming back from a long period of neglect. Ran said he was spending most of his efforts on improvements to the broader estate, investing so he and his tenants would benefit in future years. But he was clearly also bringing the house back to its former glory. The legacy from the uncle must have been every bit as large as rumour painted it.

After dinner that night, Lady Avery asked Min for some music. "I am not an accomplished pianist, my Lady," Min said.

"She sings very nicely," Mama said.

"Randall, play for Miss Bradshaw," Lady Avery commanded.

So they put their heads together to choose music, then Ran's long fingers coaxed the keys. Min remembered how they felt on her lips. And his eyes held hers as she sang:
> "Ten thousand mile it is a long way
> To leave me here alone,
> To leave me here to sigh and complain
> Where you never will hear my moans, my dear,
> Where you never will hear my moans."

And he replied, in a warm tenor:
> "Your moans, my dear, I shall never hear,
> No likewise none of your crying.
> If I go away, I'll come back again
> When from your friends you're free, my dear,
> When from your friends you're free."

They finished to applause from the mothers, whom they had quite forgotten.

"The tea tray, I think," said Lady Avery. "Ring the bell, please, Randall."

The rain had cleared the next morning, and Lady Avery insisted on riding the invalid chair to Sunday service, the rest of the party walking alongside.

Min tried to ignore the curious looks of the villagers, and focus on the performance of the chair. It handled the solid ground well, though the footman pushing it struggled when they hit soft ground.

Lady Avery was having a fine time, surrounded by people who flocked to talk to her.

"This is the first time she has taken the chair down to the village," Ran said from behind her. She felt herself warm in his direction, as if he was the sun and she a flower.

"It's a fine thing you do," Ran went on, "this chair building."

She waited. Now he would tell her that it wasn't proper for a viscountess; that she wouldn't need to continue when she was married.

Instead, he introduced her to the Vicar, and then to other people, a sea of strangers who all shook her hand, and smiled, and told her how welcome she was, and how good it was to see Lady Avery out and about.

Lady Avery took the lead on the way home, while Ran gave his right arm to Min and his left to Mama. It was good to see Lady Avery with colour in her cheeks, laughing up at Wilson the footman who was grinning back as he swerved the chair around the puddles.

"There will be no stopping her now," Ran joked. "Every fine day, she'll be running poor Wilson ragged, all over the garden and in and out of the village."

"She should be enjoying life," Mama commented. "She is a young woman, still."

"On her next birthday she'll be 41," Ran confirmed.

Min hadn't realised how young she was. She must have been little more than a child when Ran was born.

Ran was frowning a little as he watched his mother. Mama patted his arm with her free hand. "Let her enjoy herself, Lord Avery," she told him. "And you enjoy her, too, for the time you have her."

Min tried to peer around Ran. What could Mama mean?

"Did she tell you?" Ran asked.

"Yes, dear. She has had two seizures since the accident, and she has lost a little bit with each one."

"The doctor thinks…" Ran didn't finish.

"I know. She told me," Mama said. "Enjoy the time you have, dear. You are making her happy, with the work on the estate and the way you care for her."

"Randall!" Lady Avery called. "Take Mrs Bradshaw down to the gardener's cottage, my dearest, and ask them for the bulbs I promised her. Miss Bradshaw and I will wait at the lookout."

Ahead, the driveway took a curve to give a view out over the estate, Avery Hall foursquare below. Ran obeyed his instructions, and Wilson took himself a short distance away.

"I wished to speak with you, Miss Bradshaw," Lady Avery said.

Here it comes, Min thought. Now she will tell me I am not good enough for him.

"You will think me an interfering old woman, but please remember that I love my son, and I want what is best for him."

"I know that, Lady Avery."

"He wants to marry you. You know that of course."

Min nodded. She was afraid to speak in case she cried. She liked Lady Avery, and she couldn't blame her for being concerned about the same distance in status that concerned Min. But still, she could feel the tears gathering.

"I wish you would consider it, my dear. I can understand you being worried about the gossip, and I cannot promise you it will be easy, but I wanted to tell you there are two things you need never worry about."

Lady Avery paused as if to let Min comment, but Min still couldn't speak. This was so far from what she expected that she had no words. Lady Avery continued.

"You do not have to worry that Randall is like his father. He looks like his father, but he takes his nature from my family. We give our hearts once, and for a lifetime. He has given his heart to you, Miss Bradshaw. It will be yours forever.

"And, if you are concerned about living with me, do not be. I will not make old bones, though I would love to live long enough to see my grandchildren."

Min found her voice. "Lady Avery, I hope you live to be 100, and no woman in her right mind would be concerned about living with you."

"Then you will consider marrying Randall?"

Min looked down at the frail hands she'd taken in her eagerness to show Lady Avery how she esteemed her. "I am trade. He is a peer. You and I both know what Society will say."

"I do not give a fig for Society, and neither does Randall. But I understand that you must make up your own mind, my dear Minerva. I may call you Minerva, may I not?"

Chapter seven: A proposal and a proposition

Whatever Mother said to Min, she was quiet and thoughtful for the rest of the walk home. Both mothers went for a rest as soon as they'd eaten a nuncheon.

"Would you like to see the succession houses?" Candle asked Min.

He took her the long way around, through the gardens she'd not yet had a chance to see because of the rain. As he'd hoped, they were deserted. All the gardeners were with their families enjoying a Sunday rest.

Avery Hall had three succession houses. One was given over to grape vines that snaked along the walls and looped overhead, and strawberries in pots. One was growing late autumn and early spring vegetables. And in the last one, they saw the first person they'd seen since they left the house. Mugridge, the head gardener, was checking the fire that was used to keep the succession house warm.

He nodded to Candle, and smiled warmly at Min, giving her a somewhat deeper bow. The servants, who adored Mother, had taken Min to their hearts—at first for what her chairs meant to Mother, but then because she was sweet, unassuming, and genuinely interested in them.

"I be just checking this fire, my Lord, Miss. Won't be long."

Candle showed Min along the lines of seedlings—trees, shrubs, and flowers being propagated to fill the garden in spring. True to his word, Mugridge very soon said, "I be off now, then. No-one be coming this way till night time, now, my Lord. Close up when tha leaves, will 'ee?"

Candle promised, and turned back to Min. She looked both apprehensive and amused, with amusement winning.

"He thinks we want to be alone," Candle explained.

"I gathered that," she replied.

"Come. Take the chair near the stove."

It was somewhat battered, but sturdy. She sat in it and he settled himself at her feet.

It was an odd setting for a proposal, but safe. Any place he could be sure of being alone with Min in the house was a place he'd already imagined making love to her in. He wasn't confident that he could control himself if she accepted his proposal. Or even that he would get to the proposal before...

He had to stop that train of thought. The succession house was becoming less safe by the minute. He was already thinking of the logistics of lovemaking here in the dirt among the seedlings. His coat spread to protect her dress... No. Not here. Quite apart from the respect he owed to an innocent and his future viscountess, he had no intention of consummating his desire in front of a hundred glass panes.

"Min, you know what I want to ask you."

"I think I do."

"Will you, Min? Will you make me the happiest of men? Will you marry me?"

"Ran, I am not from your world."

"I know you are too good for me," he joked, "but I'm hoping you're prepared to make the sacrifice."

"Ran, I am serious. I am the daughter of a carriage maker. You are a peer. Society..."

"Min, I love you. If you love me, then Society can go hang itself."

"I want to continue making chairs."

"I hope you will."

"Really? You would not mind?"

"Min, you have a gift. I want you to use it. Say you will marry me, and I'll have the bans read. We can be wed before Christmas."

She withdrew. She didn't move a muscle, but he felt her pulling into herself, away from him.

"Don't, Randall."

His first name in full. That couldn't be good. But he wasn't Lord Avery again, which was a hopeful sign.

"Is that a no, Min?"

She shook her head.

"Is it a yes?"

Another head shake.

"Min?" He came up onto his knees in a single motion, and captured her face between both of his hands, looking into her grey eyes.

She collected herself then, his brave little goddess. "When I come back with the chair, I will give you your answer."

And then she pressed her sweet lips to his and he was lost. With a groan he enfolded her in his arms, slid his hands up behind her head, and deepened the kiss.

It could have been a minute; it could have been months. Time ceased to exist as he explored her mouth and she followed his lead. Her tentative movements, bold and shy at the same time, intoxicated him and he was conscious of nothing but the burning need to sink into her softness. Until a piece of gravel on the path turned as he shifted his knee, and dug into his skin.

He drew away from her with a groan.

Had he done that? Her lips were swollen and red, a sleeve was pulled down baring her shoulder, and one glorious breast was nearly tipped out of her dress. Another nudge, and he'd see...

He blinked, and shook the idea out of his head. "Min, my own dearest love." He had to be calm. She looked as dazed as he felt. Probably more so, given her innocence. If his world was shaken, hers must be reeling.

"I would help you put yourself to rights, beloved. But I don't dare touch you."

She straightened her dress, repinned the lace cap she wore in her hair, rewrapped her shawl around her, all the while sneaking peeks at him and colouring each time their eyes met.

Before they left the succession house, he put a finger on her now clothed arm.

"Min, will you accept my apology, beloved? I meant no disrespect, I promise you. I should never have kissed you. I know how powerfully I react when we touch."

To his surprise, she suddenly grinned. "Ah but Ran, you forget. I kissed you first."

Daniel must have left Bath before dawn. He was at the door by mid-morning, and wouldn't accept Ran's invitation to stop for lunch. Rain was coming, he said, and he wanted to be safely back in Bath before the deluge.

Min, her valise packed with all the notes and drawings she needed to finish the chair, kissed Lady Avery on the cheek, and gave Ran her hand. He lifted it and deliberately placed a kiss in the palm.

"Bring it back to me, Min," he said.

She almost told him, then and there, that she would marry him, but—no. She had to get back to Bath. She would make her decision without his disturbing presence tugging her to fall into his arms.

Neither Daniel nor Mama commented on the kiss. Mama asked after Papa, and then she and Daniel discussed the dispatches about the Navy's victory. They were calling it the

Battle of Trafalgar, and nearly 450 British sailors had died. Almost ten times as many died on the other side.

Min didn't contribute. Mostly, she didn't listen. She sat and thought about chair design, and what she needed to do to finish Candle's chair for his mother in time for Christmas.

And all the while her thoughts kept going back to Candle's kiss, and to the answer she would need to give him.

Min strode across the yard, her patens sending sprays of water flying from puddles she ignored in her indignation. Daniel was in the outer office. She didn't trust herself to speak in front of the clerk; she jerked her head towards the inner office, and went through to wait for him.

He was quick to join her, his face wary. "Now, Minnie, what's got your back up?"

"Did you tell…" She caught herself. Took a deep breath. Best to check the facts first.

"Richards has ignored the instructions I left, redrawn my designs, and reworked the chairs for the Barfoot sale. He claims he had your authorisation."

Her cousin's eyes gave him away, sliding evasively to one side. "Now, Minnie. Richards is a good foreman."

"You gave him authorisation to change my work," she said flatly.

"He's highly experienced, Minnie. He said a few changes would save materials and increase our profit."

"A few changes that mean we do not meet the client's specifications and will not make the sale."

"You are exaggerating. He showed me his drawings. Sound carriage design."

"Unsound chair design," she snapped back.

Papa entered the room, saw the two of them, and closed the door behind him.

"What's going on?"

"I want Richards out of my workshop," Min told Papa, not taking her eyes off Daniel.

"She is upset about a few economies that I approved." Daniel put on his 'I am reasonable and you are a female' voice. "Look, Minnie, you have to let go and let us take over. After all, you will leave all this behind you when you marry your Viscount."

"Point one," Min thought she did well to keep her voice calm and level, "I have not accepted Lord Avery's proposal. Point two, if I do accept, he has promised that I can continue making chairs. Point three, the chair workshop is mine, and you had no right to allow Richards to disobey a direct instruction."

"Well, Minerva. Strictly speaking Daniel is general manager of the whole works," Papa said. The traitor.

She looked at the two of them in silence for a moment. First things first. She needed to deal with the chair disaster.

"Let me explain the problem, gentlemen. Richards has scaled down standard carriage parts." Blank looks. "Scaled them precisely. Without any consideration of the structural integrity of the new thicknesses."

The two men exchanged glances again. Consternation had replaced smug commiseration. Just so, she thought with a grim satisfaction.

"All three chairs will need to be remade if we are not to forego 90 guineas and the chance of future orders. And I am fully committed on Lady Avery's chair." Fortunately, Richards had left that chair alone. She had made every inch of it herself, investing hours. She didn't just want efficient engineering; she wanted a superb piece of furniture. Carved, turned, and polished woodwork for the handle; upholstery in the finest leather with a buttoned back and seat, sewn detail, and cording on the edges.

"I'll see to it, Minnie." Daniel sounded humble, but she couldn't expect that to last. She was so used to his persistent belief in his male superiority that she noticed it only because of the contrast with Ran's respect.

"Very well then. And Richards goes."

"I'll reassign him."

"Thank you." She could be gracious in victory.

She left her menfolk in the office they shared. She wanted to cut the leather for the arms and leave it to relax, and add another coat of polish to the handle. It could be drying while she went out to tea with Cara and her friends. She was cautiously venturing into Society, and finding it less threatening than she expected.

Bother. She had forgotten to tell her father that she wouldn't be walking home with him.

Turning back through the outer office, she started to push the inner door open, and paused.

"Do you think Lord Avery means to let Minnie make her chairs?" That was Daniel.

"Don't be daft. Whoever heard of a viscountess doing that sort of stuff? No he's just saying it. Or he means it now, but will come to his senses soon enough." That was Papa.

"Yes. You should have put a stop to it long ago, Uncle."

"It made her happy. And she's done some good work, you can't deny it."

"It isn't right, though. A woman shouldn't be doing carriage work, Uncle. I'm sorry to hear that Lord Avery is encouraging her."

"You know what they say, lad: 'When a man grows hard between the thighs, he grows soft between the ears.' He's soft on my girl, right enough."

Min had heard enough. Her ears burning, she retreated to her workshop.

Were they right? Ran had sounded so convincing when he spoke of his hope that she would continue her work. But she had always known that marriage would make her dependent on the goodwill of a husband, and the face a man showed before marriage was not always the one his wife saw after.

Could Ran be trusted?

The flowers continued to arrive, and so did presents of produce from Avery Hall. Min didn't need the constant reminders. Ran was a phantom presence wherever she went. Everything she saw or heard, she wanted to share with him. Ran would like this. Ran would find that funny. Ran would be interested.

The nights were worse. Ran had woken something in her. She didn't know how to ease whatever he had aroused, but she knew who could ease it.

And all the time, Ran's view of her chair making, and her father's opinion of that view, warred in her head.

One morning, the note with the day's present went beyond the usual compliments, adding:

"I beg Mrs Bradshaw and Miss Bradshaw to do me the honour of accepting my escort to the Lower Assembly Rooms this evening."

Min had been planning to go—the next step in her experiment in social climbing. But going with Ran would be wonderful. Mama sent a note back with the Avery servant, inviting Ran to dinner, and Min hurried to the workshop to make an early start on the day's work.

Ran was in Bath! Min half expected to see him on her walk to work. She almost stayed in her walking dress, in case he came to her workshop, but common sense prevailed and she donned her overalls.

She would see him tonight. Tonight, she could tell him all the things she had been saving up to say, and she could hear about his week at Avery Hall, and about Lady Avery, and the planned gardens, and the performance of the chair, and the progress of the renovations...

Min caught herself. When had her life begun to revolve around this man and his concerns?

Suddenly, he was there. "Min."

She dropped her tools and walked into his open arms for a kiss that satisfied and, at the same time, left her longing for more. All too soon, he put her gently from him.

"Min, I won't stay. But I couldn't wait to see you. Have you been well? You look well."

"Yes. And you?"

"I'm well now," Ran said, and the warmth in his eyes said much more. "I must go. I have appointments today... I will see you tonight, Min."

One more kiss, and he was gone. So much for keeping her head until she had made her decision.

After daydreaming for an hour, Min packed up and went home. She was accomplishing nothing today.

Candle was humming to himself as he walked into the White Hart after seeing the Bradshaw ladies home. The evening had been wonderful. The dancing, the conversation, the food, everything had conspired to provide a perfect evening. And, at the centre of it all, his Minerva.

She was his, he was almost sure of it. He hadn't asked her again, but tonight she'd had her armour down. She'd been happy to be with him; she'd let her hand linger on his in the dance, and she'd leant into him when he'd offered his arm to go in to supper. Two dances had not been nearly enough; Candle would have taken every dance, given a choice.

But he'd played at being civilised, even danced with other females, although there was only one in the room worth thinking about.

Surely she was planning to say yes? Her father thought so, but her mother warned him not to be too certain. And in the light of what her cousin had let slip, Candle was more and more sure that it might take his secret plan to convince his Min she could trust her future to him.

Candle stopped at the desk to see if there had been any messages, and waited while the clerk checked.

"Candle, old man."

"Michaels; good to see you."

His friend grinned. "I saw you at the assembly, but you didn't have eyes for anyone but that black-haired beauty you were escorting. Gorgeous female. Lovely..." He cupped both hands in front of his chest and jiggled them up and down.

"The future Lady Avery," Candle warned. The clerk was shaking his head. No messages.

Michaels said a cheerful, "Sorry," but was not at all abashed. "When's the happy day?"

"She hasn't accepted me yet. But she will." If he said it often enough, perhaps it would be true.

"I imagine she will," his friend agreed. "Candle Avery, the man who never gives up. Look, Candle, I thought you might have those volunteer training plans you promised me."

"They're up in my room; come on up and I'll give them to you."

They were discussing the most recent news from the Fleet as Candle opened the door to his room and led the way in.

"Will you have a drink?" Candle asked, crossing to the decanter on the sideboard.

"Uh, Candle." Michaels was stock still in the middle of the room, his face suddenly neutral. He was staring at the bed.

"Candle, darling, come back to bed." Lady Norton, her hair hanging down across her shoulders, sat up in his bed. A sheet preserved some shreds of decency, but she was clearly naked. Very naked.

Candle was suddenly coldly furious. "You mistake, madam. I would sooner bed a snake."

"But Candle! After the afternoon we had?"

The door opened again, and Kitteridge burst in. "What are you doing with my sister, you villain?" he declaimed, then frowned at Michaels. "He isn't meant to be here."

Lady Norton struck her forehead with the back of one hand. "Guy! Candle, we are discovered! My brother knows all!"

Candle suppressed a laugh. High melodrama indeed! Though it would be quite unfunny if he had come up to bed on his own, or if he didn't have witnesses to how he'd spent his afternoon and evening.

"Michaels, shut the door, will you? We'll keep this to ourselves if we can."

"You have compromised my sister! I demand satisfaction." Clearly Kitteridge intended to follow the script despite the unexpected addition to the cast.

"Very well," Candle said. "Michaels, will you stand my second?"

"Not a duel. Marriage. You're meant to marry her," Kitteridge explained.

"No," Candle said.

"But she's in your bed. You have to marry her." Kitteridge was pleading now.

"Kitteridge, I have been in company every minute of the day since I arrived in Bath. I have witnesses who will swear to that. The only one to suffer if you and Lady Norton insist on making a scandal is Lady Norton."

He turned, then, and locked eyes with Lady Norton, but continued to address Kitteridge. "I don't know whether your sister is after my money or if she is with child again, but I will not be her dupe."

Lady Norton shrieked at the suggestion she might be pregnant. "Guy! He has insulted me! Call him out!"

"But Vivi, he has been a soldier. He's probably a good shot."

"Regimental champion three years running," Michaels offered. He was bouncing forward on his feet, like a boy on outskirts of a fistfight: close enough to see the blood but preserved from any pain and having a wonderful time. "And he's none too bad with a sword."

Kitteridge nodded vigorously, and said, "He's good with his fists, too. You should have seen him at school. He'd go into this sort of calm rage, and nothing would stop him."

"I've seen it," Michaels agreed. "A sort of cold, logical berserker. Very scary. I wouldn't duel with him if I were you."

Candle was keeping an eye on Lady Norton. She was assessing every object within reach. He recognised the signs. He'd had a mistress who threw things when she was upset.

Yes. There went the jug, water and all. He'd been ready to duck, but obviously she was angrier with her brother.

The jug struck a glancing blow, and what water hadn't already soaked the bed and sprayed across the floor finished up on Kitteridge's jacket.

"Vivi!" he complained, "I hope that doesn't stain."

"Mr Michaels and I are going downstairs," Candle told them. "We will return in 30 minutes, bringing the manager with us. I suggest the two of you leave before that time. And Lady Norton, Michaels and I will keep this to ourselves. But only if you do not try anything like it again."

They didn't speak as they descended the stairs. Candle ordered a brandy each, and they took it to a corner of the public room. "Well," Michaels said. "You do know how to make an evening entertaining, old chap."

Chapter eight: A Christmas present

The chair was done. It was, perhaps, the best Min had ever made. It was wrapped in protective blankets and secured to the top of the carriage that would take her and Mama to Avery Hall the following day.

As she sat with Cara in the tea rooms at the Roman Baths, waiting for Lady Cresthover to return from the retiring room, Min was thinking about the answer she would give Ran. She had done a great deal of thinking in the last two weeks.

She was no longer afraid of going into Society. Oh, the high sticklers and the bullies might never accept her. But enough of her old schoolmates had become friends that she need not fear isolation. She would never be a darling of the ton, but neither did she wish to be.

And she had learned that she could ignore any nasty remarks made to her. They no longer had the power to crush her, even without Ran's support. If he stood at her side, she could face anything.

Ran at her side. That was the biggest lesson of all. Whether he meant what he said about her chairs or not, she was going to accept Ran. If she had to make a choice between her work or her love, she chose love. With him, she felt complete. His absence felt like a gaping hole in her personal universe. She could, if she must, do something other than build chairs. She could not contemplate facing the rest of her life without Ran.

"You are thinking about Lord Avery again, are you not?" Cara said.

"Is it so obvious?"

"You are just like Henrietta Millworthy. She loved the man she married, too. And before the wedding she used to drift off into nowhere, just like you." Cara reached across the table and grasped Min's hands. "Marry him, Min. Do not let cats like my cousin stop you."

Min laughed a little. "I plan to, Cara."

"And you will still be my friend, will you not?" Cara looked a little lost. "I will miss you when you move away from Bath."

"I will write, and I will not be far away. I imagine we will be able to visit, you and I."

"Well, is this not sweet? My cousin and her little shop-girl friend." Lady Norton, her voice pitched to carry across the room, sneered down at them.

"I suppose you think you are so smart, Mini Bradshaw, trapping a peer. But you will never fit in. Do you hear me? Never."

"Lady Norton, this is a private conversation," Min said.

"He will not be faithful to you, you know. His father was notorious for his affairs. Ask her mother." Lady Norton pointed a gloved finger at Cara. "Everyone knows her mother was one of his amours, when she was just plain Sally Hemple. He had a taste for a bit of the common, just like his son."

Min met Lady Cresthover's shocked eyes over Lady Norton's shoulder and attempted to stem the flow. "Lady Norton, that is quite enough."

Lady Norton took no notice. "Sally Hemple. My mother told me that she trapped my uncle. Just like you are trapping poor Lord Avery, Miss Bradshaw." She gave her cousin a poke with one finger. "You should try it, Carrie darling. Before you crumble to dust on the shelf, you poor old thing." She swayed a little. "Ooops." She caught herself by grabbing the back of a chair, and laughed her tinkling laugh.

Lady Cresthover was whispering to a footman, who nodded and hurried away.

"He is not very good in bed, Miss Bradshaw. You should not hope for much. Perhaps you could get my Auntie to give him a few pointers?"

The footman was back, with a colleague. Lady Norton yelped as they took an elbow each.

"How dare you! Unhand me. Do you know who I am?"

She was continuing to protest as they half carried her out of the room. "A very sad case," Lady Cresthover said in a carrying voice. "A sad unsteadiness in her mother's family, you know." She dropped into a piercing whisper that could be heard in every corner of the room. "It is said that her grandfather thought he was an elephant."

"Come, Cara, Miss Bradshaw." Ignoring the embarrassed titters, she sailed out of the room, Min and Cara in her wake, and Polly the maid scurrying behind.

In the foyer, Lady Cresthover ordered Lady Norton into a sedan chair. "It will keep her out of the public eye," she said, her voice back at its normal volume. "Miss Bradshaw, do not be concerned about my niece. She will retiring to a quiet place in the country." She turned away to follow her daughter and the chair, then turned back again. "And I can assure you that young Lord Avery is nothing like his father."

The men worked all night by lantern light to finish Candle's surprise. He was tempted to wait until she had given him her answer and then show her. He would love her to choose him without his gift. But no. He wouldn't play games, and wouldn't take the risk she'd turn him down and then refuse to change her mind.

He would show her first, and then propose to her again.

He checked the surprise for the third time that morning, ran inside again to see if a message had arrived from the gate yet, stopped to ask his mother how she was, and went back out to the steps to see if he could see their carriage.

The weather was cold, with gusty showers that hinted at sleet in their future. He hoped Bradshaw's carriage was warm. What was he thinking! The man was the king of carriages. He would send his womenfolk in the best he had.

Returning inside, Candle looked around the entry hall. Yes. It looked splendid. Mother loved Christmas, and took no notice of the tradition that decorations must wait until Christmas Eve. As soon as the Christmas Octave started on the 17th of December, she mobilised the entire household to transform the house into a Christmas paradise. The servants had outdone themselves this year. Every surface sported ivy, holly, and greenery. More greenery was tied to the stair balustrade with bright ribbons, and ribbons festooned the kissing balls of holly, ivy, rosemary, and mistletoe. Mother had made enough kissing boughs to put one in every room, upstairs and down.

"My Lord, she be here! Her carriage be coming down the hill."

Candle waited impatiently at the bottom of the steps, and was at the carriage door as soon as it rolled to a stop. The door swung open before he could grasp the handle, and Min tumbled out into his arms.

"Yes," she said. "Yes, Ran, yes. I will marry you."

Later, after he had kissed her, been kissed on the cheek by Mrs Bradshaw, and escorted them inside to his mother for congratulations and more kisses, he managed to detach Min from the admiring group around the new chair.

"I have something for you, beloved. A surprise present for Christmas. Mother, Mrs Bradshaw, I am taking Min to show her her present."

The mothers waved them away.

Ran refused to tell her what the surprise was, but he took her outside, and to a building behind the stable. "Stop." he commanded. He rushed ahead and opened the door, then returned and covered her eyes with his hands. "I'll guide you. Take three paces forward. Now turn slightly and take one more pace. Now feel forward with your foot for the step. There are three steps. One; two; three. Two more paces. Stop."

He removed his hands.

Min stared. Then turned her head. Then turned in a complete circle.

"Ran? Ran, it's my workshop." She ran forward and brushed her hand over the drafting table, picked up and put down the pens and pencils waiting for her, straightened the blotter. Next, the workbench, where racks waited for her tools, still back in Bath in the racks he'd duplicated. The shelves of supplies were mostly empty, too, but she could imagine them filled.

"Ran." She smiled at him and his dear features wavered as her eyes swam with tears.

He looked concerned. "Min? Is it alright?"

"It is the most wonderful thing anyone has every done for me. My workshop."

"How else are you going to keep inventing your wonderful chairs, my love?"

"Ran." That seemed to be the only word she could say, but she invested it with a wealth of meaning. Then she melted into his arms, and neither of them spoke for some time.

Candle Avery was climbing the hill track in the rain. He was cold, wet, and thoroughly happy.

He and his companions had refused a lift on the cart taking the freshly cut yule log back to Avery Hall. The hill track was the quicker way. And at the Hall Min waited for him. Min Avery. His wife of three days.

He'd be hard put to pick the happiest moment of his life. When she tumbled out of the coach and accepted his proposal? When she agreed to using the special licence he'd obtained, and to marrying him as soon as her family could come from Bath? When he'd turned from his place before the altar and seen her walking towards him in a cloud of lace, or a few minutes later when she'd given him her hand and her trust with her vows? When she welcomed him into her embrace and her body later that night? When he woke up the next morning to her shy suggestion that they should make love again?

Each day, he fell in love a little more.

They crested the top and Daniel said something Candle didn't catch. Michaels gave Candle a friendly punch on the arm. "No point in talking to him," he told Daniel. "The man walks around in a daze."

"To be fair, we are intruding on his honeymoon," Daniel noted.

To be fair, they were mostly being careful not to intrude. But it was Christmas Eve, and it was his job as master of the house to collect the yule log. "My wife and I want you to enjoy your Christmas in our home," he said. As well as Min's family, Michaels and Miss Cresthover had come for the wedding, and were staying for Christmas.

"Preferably without disturbing you and your wife. Yes, we understand," said the irrepressible Daniel.

Michaels gestured ahead. "Who, if I do not mistake, is coming to meet us."

Below, two women waited in the shelter of the summerhouse.

Sure enough, as the men drew level with the structure, Miss Cresthover and the new Lady Avery dashed down the steps under their umbrellas.

"So do we have a good yule log," Min asked.

"An excellent one," Daniel said, "but I'm sorry to say we failed in one mission." He let his eyes, lips and shoulders droop.

"What was that?" Cara could be depended on to ask the questions that set Daniel up for whatever punchline he intended to deliver.

Candle held Min back, letting the others go on ahead, but they could still hear Daniel's reply as the three in the lead turned the corner of the path.

"We couldn't find any mistletoe to replace all the berries Min and Candle have used, so nobody else in the Hall can be kissed, Miss Cresthover."

"But Mr Whitlow, you kissed me this morning!" replied Cara.

"I kissed you this morning," Candle told Min.

"Really? I am not sure that I remember. Perhaps if you do it again?"

After several minutes, he drew his head back. "Min, the yule log won't be here for another hour. Shall we go up to bed?"

"Up the stairs in front of our friends and family? Ran, I could not."

He thought for a moment of suggesting the back stairs, but through the kitchen full of servants wouldn't appeal to her, either.

"However," said Min, "your study has a sofa and a warm fire, and I unlatched the window before I came out."

"Ah, Min," Candle told her, "how lucky I am to have a clever wife."

THE END

Thank you for reading my novella. If you enjoyed it, I hope you will take a moment to leave me a review at your favourite online retailer. Please feel free to share *Candle's Christmas Chair* with your friends.

Candle and Min first appeared when I was writing my novel *Farewell to Kindness*. I needed someone to diagnose sabotage on an invalid chair that collapsed in the middle of an assembly, and Min pushed her way out of the crowd, with Candle hovering protectively behind her.

I wondered how two such different people got together, and this story is the result.

Below, you will find a brief summary of the language of flowers, a sample of *Farewell to Kindness*, to be published in April 2015, a description of other books I'm working on, my brief biography, and places you can find me online. Please read on.

News and special offers

Subscribe to my newsletter for news about publication dates and more. As a subscriber, you will receive advance information about cover designs, book trailers, book blurbs, release dates, and special price periods. You'll also get exclusive subscriber-only special offers, including articles, short stories, and competitions.

I don't expect to send a newsletter more than a dozen times a year, so don't fear that I'll clutter up your inbox. http://judeknightauthor.com/newsletter/

Acknowledgements

Thank you to my beta readers, Sue, Carol, and Angela. You read my story in record time, and came back with comments and suggestions that helped me make it stronger. Thank you, husband of mine, for endless cups of coffee and tea, and wine in the evenings, for feeding me, and for dragging me from the keyboard occasionally to remind me I am in the 21st century, not the 19th. Thank you also to all the other people who have encouraged me on this journey. I appreciate every one of you.

Thank you to Britt Leveridge, who drew the chair featured on the cover. Britt, you did an amazing job. The background picture is 'A view of King's Weston in the snow' photographed by Stephen Burns and released into the public domain under a Creative Commons Licence. Thanks, Stephen Burns.

Say it with flowers

The language of flowers has a history stretching back to antiquity. Many cultures around the world have developed their own symbolism of flowers, but the symbolism known in the west mostly traces back to the harems of the Ottoman Empire.

In the early 18th Century, Charles II, King of Sweden, after living for five years in Turkey, brought the language of flowers back to Europe. Lady Mary Wortley Montague, wife of the English ambassador to Constantinople, also became fascinated with the way the ladies of the court used flowers to pass coded messages, and introduced the language of flowers to England. (Though Ophelia's ramblings in Shakespeare's Hamlet hint that some meanings predate this introduction.)

In 1805, when Candle was sending his gifts, the language of flowers was well known, but not yet as popular as it became in the Victorian era, when several books were published giving common meanings.

Here are the flowers Candle used.
> Anemones: fragile or forsaken
> Asters: symbol of love
> Carnations in general: fascination (a solid colour means yes and striped means no)
> Carnations, red: admiration
> Carnations, white: sweet and lovely, pure love
> Daisies: innocence
> Ferns: sincerity, fascination
> Holly: domestic happiness
> Hollyhocks: ambition
> Irises: your friendship means so much to me
> Ivy: faithfulness, wedded love
> Lilly of the valley: sweetness, humility
> Mimosa: sensitivity
> Myrtle: love, marriage
> Orchids: beauty
> Rosebuds, moss: confessions of love
> Rosemary: remembrance
> Roses, Christmas: anxiety
> Roses, damask: ambassador of love
> Roses, tea: I'll remember, always
> Roses, white: innocence
> Roses, yellow: joy, friendship

Salvia, blue: thoughts
Stephanotis: happiness in marriage
Zinnias: thinking of an absent friend

No doubt in another season he will give Min:
Camellias: admiration, perfection
Camellias, pink: longing for you
Camellias, red: you're a flame in my heart
Camellias, white: you're adorable
Chrysanthemums, red: I love
Chrysanthemums, white: truth
Daffodils: regard, you're the only one
Dandelions: faithfulness, happiness
Forget-me-nots: true love, memories
Forsythia: anticipation
Gardenias: you are lovely
Heather, lavender: admiration
Heather, white: protection
Hyacinths, blue: constancy
Hyacinths, pink: play
Jonquils: love me
Lillies, calla: beauty
Lillies, yellow: I'm walking on air
Primroses: I can't live without you
Roses, coral: desire
Stock: constant affection
Sweet peas: blissful pleasure (also goodbye, and thank
you for a lovely time)
Tulips, red: declaration of love
Violets: modesty
Violets, white: let's take a chance on happiness

But we can believe he will never need:
Bachelor buttons: single blessedness
Bouquet of withered flowers: rejected love
Carnations, yellow: you have disappointed me
Chrysanthemums, yellow: slighted love
Dead leaves: sadness
Geraniums: stupidity, folly
Hyacinths, purple: I am sorry, please forgive me
Hyacinths, yellow: jealousy
Hydrangeas: frigidity, vanity, heartlessness
Lillies, orange: hatred
Marigolds: cruelty, grief

Monkshood: beware of the deadly foe
Petunias: resentment, anger
Roses, dark crimson: mourning
Snapdragons: deception

Farewell to Kindness

Available from Amazon.

For three years, Rede has been searching Canada for those who ordered the murders of his wife and children.

Now back in England, he has inherited an Earldom from his cousin George, and is close to finding the investors who ordered the deaths in an attempt to destroy Rede's fur trading enterprise. He travels to his country estate in Longford, West Gloucestershire, to be close to the investigation.

He does not need the distraction of an overwhelming longing for the lovely widow who lives in one of the cottages he owns. A widow, moreover, with a small daughter whose distinctive eyes mark her as George's child.

For six years, from the night Anne blackmailed George at arrow-point for an income and a place to live, she has been in hiding with her sisters and daughter.

She hides from the scandal of her daughter's conception. More importantly, she hides from the Earl of Selby, who has sinister plans for the sisters. He no longer has legal rights as guardian to the older sisters, but the youngest sister is still only 18. He cannot be allowed to find her.

The last thing Anne needs is an inconvenient attraction to the local Earl. Rede is everything she has learned not to trust: a man, a peer, a Redepenning. If he finds out who she is, she may lose everything.

As their attraction builds against a backdrop of the village Whitsun Week festivities, several accidents make Rede believe his enemies have found him, and leads Anne to wonder whether Selby has found her.

Prologue
London, 1801

He was drunk. But not nearly drunk enough. He still saw his young friend's dying eyes everywhere. In half-caught glimpses of strangers reflected in windows along Bond Street, under the hats of coachmen that passed him along the silent streets to Bedford Square, in the flickering lamps that shone pallidly against the cold London dawn as he stumbled up the steps to his front door.

They followed his every waking hour: hot, angry, hate-filled eyes that had once been warm with admiration.

He drank to forget, but all he could do was remember.

One more flight of stairs, then through the half open door to his private sitting room, already reaching for the waiting decanter of brandy as he crossed the floor.

He had a glass of oblivion halfway to his lips before he noticed the painting.

It stood on an easel, lit by a carefully arranged tree of candles. His own face was illuminated – the golden shades of his hair, his intensely blue eyes. The artist had captured his high cheekbones and sculpted jaw. "One of London's most beautiful men," he'd been called.

He stalked to the easel, moving with great care to avoid spilling his drink.

Yes. The artist had talent. Who could have given him such a thing?

As he bent forward to look at it more closely, something whipped past his face. With a solid thunk, an arrow struck the painting, to stand quivering between the painted eyes.

He dropped his glass as he started backwards, flailing to keep his balance, and trying to turn at the same time to see behind him. There. In the shadows behind the door. A silent gowned figure with another arrow already nocked and ready to fly.

"Who are you? What do you want?" The drink thickened his voice. "If I shout, I'll wake the whole household."

"The household are all either below stairs or well above. And you will have, at most, one shout before I put this arrow between your eyes. I have demonstrated I can." It was a woman's voice, low and determined.

He glanced back at the arrow, and swallowed.

"You won't shoot me. You're a woman."

"I will shoot you with pleasure, if I must," the woman said. "But shooting you is not my first choice."

He pulled himself straight, glaring. "You won't get away with this. Don't you know who I am?"

"You do not know who I am, do you? I am the woman you owe a future to. And I mean to collect. You will give me either my future or my revenge."

He took a step towards her, leaning forward to peer into the shadows. She lifted the arrow point fractionally, saying, "No closer!"

He stopped. "I don't even know who you are. What crime have I supposedly committed? What do you want from me?"

She gestured to the chair by the fire with the point of her arrow. "Sit," she commanded, and once he complied, she moved out into the light. "Now do you know who I am?"

She looked familiar. But no, he couldn't place her. He shook his head.

She was silent for a moment. When she spoke, her voice was stiff with outrage. "Perhaps I can help your memory. You killed my brother. You sank my reputation into the gutter. You left me with sisters to care for and a baby to raise. Remember me now, guardian?" She sounded like a heroine from a Gothic novel. Come to think of it, it was a Gothic novel, and he was the villain.

"You're Stockie's sister." His voice was resigned. Really, he might have guessed that Stockie would find a corporeal way to haunt him. "But wait; you don't understand. I didn't mean to kill your brother. I was drunk. I misfired. You can't blame me for that."

She said nothing.

"He challenged me. I had to meet him. It was a matter of honour. I didn't mean to kill him."

She looked at him coldly. "I am not here to discuss the past. I want somewhere to live; somewhere in the country where you do not go. On the table at your elbow is a letter to your land steward in Gloucestershire. It tells him to give me and my sisters life tenancy of a suitable cottage, with sufficient land to feed us. Read it. Sign it. Then toss it over here to me."

He frowned, drawing his brows together. "But your cousin said he'd take care of everything."

"He told you what he had planned?"

"That he would find you a place to live until the baby was born, and make sure there was no scandal."

"That he would lock us two older girls away, sell the baby, and marry our little sister to his loathsome son."

He'd met the son. He wouldn't put a dog he didn't like in that boy's care. He had given her dying brother his promise that he'd leave the girls alone, but surely Stockie would expect him to come to their rescue?

"Then let me see to it. I am your guardian. And your trustee."

"We do not want you. And we do not want our cousin and his plans. Just leave us alone."

He examined his feet, ashamed to meet her scornful eyes. "I didn't mean to hurt anybody. I was drunk. I wasn't thinking."

"Sign the papers."

"I am sorry, you know."

"'Sorry' does nothing. If you are sorry, sign the papers."

He reached for the papers; began to read.

"And do not think to renege on the bargain," she went on. "A cottage and some money for us to live on to make it possible for me to look after my family, and I will go away and be quiet about what you did. But if you try to take back the cottage, or to harm any one of us, I will make sure the whole of society knows.

"Do not think I am afraid to speak," she added, as he opened his mouth to tell her she had nothing to fear. "You have made certain our place in Society is lost. Take away what little we have left, and I will take you down with me. I know Society blames the innocent maid rather than the rake that ruins her, but they will care that she was your ward; they will care that you killed another ward, her own brother."

"Look; I've signed." He rolled the papers and tossed them at her feet. "You said you want money. I... I'll give you a letter for my bank. How much?"

She gestured with her head towards the purse he'd dropped as he came in the door. "What is in that?"

"My winnings from tonight."

"It looked heavy."

"I had a run of luck. Three thousand guineas, more or less."

"I will take it."

He frowned. "Three thousand? Will that be enough?"

"With the cottage, it will be enough. I don't want anything else from you except your absence from our lives."

"I'm still your guardian."

"For the sake of us all, I suggest you forget that. I will look after my sisters now."

He couldn't meet her eyes. He studied his hands, instead. What if he broke his promise to Stockie?

"I could marry you. That would fix things."

She shook her head, looking at him with contempt, then said, "Take off all your clothes."

He gave a surprised laugh; one that turned automatically to a leer. "Sweetheart..."

She drew the bowstring that she'd allowed to relax, reaiming the arrow at his heart. "All your clothes. Now. Take them off... Gather them together... Good. Now throw them out the window."

Even through the drink; even at the point of an arrow, the thought of being naked in front of this woman caused a little stirring in the portion of his anatomy that had caused the problem. Her face was fiery red. Showing and then undoing his corset was embarrassing. More and more, in his casual liaisons, he was disrobing in the dark. His mistresses, of course, made no comment about his growing paunch.

He obeyed her instructions, opening the window and leaning out to drop his clothes. The bundle unfurled and spilled down the front steps into the street. Behind him, he heard the door shut, and the key turn in the lock.

Without much hope, he tried the door, and then the door to the bedroom. Both were locked. She hadn't missed a trick.

He wished her every success. Perhaps another letter to his land steward, instructing that she be given every care? No. That would only draw attention to her. Better let her handle it.

It was chilly in the room. It could be hours before the valet tried the door. But he had most of a decanter of brandy to keep the cold and the ghost at bay.

Perhaps, if he stayed away from Longford and kept the girls' secrets, his betrayed friend would stop haunting him?

Other books by Jude Knight

A Raging Madness*: Book 2 of *The Golden Redepennings Coming December 2015
When Alex Redepenning, formerly of the 20th Light Dragoons, comes to the funeral of Ella Melville's mother-in-law, he does not expect Ella to turn up in his bedroom at the nearby inn, seeking help. They have met twice in the last 10 years; once when she married one of Alex's fellow officers under dubious circumstances, and once when she arrived too late to attend her husband's death bed. And they parted rancorously each time.

After what he said at their last meeting, Ella hoped never to see Alex again; even though he has been her hero since she was a girl of 15. But an overheard conversation between her brother-in-law and his wife leaves her with no-one else to turn to. She wants Alex's help to escape those who would keep her prisoner and have her declared insane. Then she wants him to go away and leave her alone.

But danger follows them; Ella's in-laws want her confined, and someone Alex annoyed seems to want him dead. Joining forces is sensible. If they can survive their enemies, the only risk is to their hearts.

Encouraging Prudence*: Book 1 of *The Virtue Sisters Coming September 2015
David and Prudence, operatives for one of England's shadowy spymasters, are sent to investigate a spying ring that is stealing secrets for the French by blackmailing aristocrats. Among those they investigate are David's legitimate brothers (the sons of the Duke who sired him) and the husband of one of Prue's three sisters.

After what happened last time they worked together, both David and Prue are determined they won't surrender to the strong physical attraction between them. They're professionals. They'll find the blackmailer and the spy behind him, and part again.

And, since they have to go to Bristol as part of the investigation, they might as well also carry out an inquiry for one of David's friends, Stephen Redepenning, the new Earl of Chirbury.

It is not until the danger that lurks in Bristol takes Prue from him that David realises what she means to him. And finding her again may mean choosing between his country and his woman.

Lord Danwood's Dilemma: **Book 1 of** *Danwood's Daughters* Coming April 2016

Inheriting from a distant cousin who had no sons, Anthony Simon Wentworth, the new Earl of Danwood, finds that his predecessor had a unique way of stacking the odds so that a grandson of his would one day be Earl. Tony has inherited the title and the entailed land, but has no way to support it. To win the non-entailed wealth, he must wed and get with child one of the former Lord Danwood's eight daughters.

The legitimate daughters live at Danwood Castle in the North York Moors. In a nearby coastal village, the former Earl kept a second family by his wife's sister (now deceased). The eldest daughter, Sophia, keeps life on an even keel for her two sisters and two brothers, despite a lack of money and the general disapproval of the village.

Tony thinks he will settle the mistress's children somewhere out of sight and marry one of the legitimate children. But he is distracted by the need to rescue his new relatives from smugglers, the coastguard, an angry farmer or two, the machinations of their aunt, and his growing appreciation of the feisty Sophia.

Connect with Jude Knight

Jude Knight is the pen name of Judy Knighton.

After a career in commercial writing, editing, and publishing, I am returning to my first love, fiction. I love capable determined heroines, and heroes who appreciate them.

My first novel is *Farewell to Kindness*, number one in *The Golden Redepennings*, publication date 1 April 2015. I have several novels in progress, and plot outlines for 40+, all set in the early 19th century. The plans include seven series, several stand-alone novels, novellas, and short stories, and a number of characters who intersect across series.

Follow me on Twitter:
http://twitter.com/JudeKnightBooks
Friend me on Facebook:
http://facebook.com/judeknightbooks
Subscribe to my blog: http://judeknightauthor.com
Subscribe to my newsletter:
http://judeknightauthor.com/newsletter/
Follow me on Goodreads:
http://www.goodreads.com/judeknight